"The shirt has to go."

Heat seared a path through her, heading south to her core. "It'll have to do for now. I don't have another."

Jake stepped back. "You can have mine."

When Alex turned to face him, a protest on her lips, she stopped, her thoughts flying out of her head as Jake unclipped the fasteners on his vest and lowered it to the ground.

Her mouth went dry and her palms filled with sweat. "What are you doing?"

He smiled. "Giving you my shirt. Granted, it might be a little sweaty, but it will be better than what you have on."

He unbuttoned his uniform jacket and slipped out of it. Then he yanked his T-shirt up over his head in one fluid, ever-so-sexy move.

FIVE WAYS TO SURRENDER

New York Times Bestselling Author
ELLE JAMES

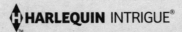

To my daughters for being such strong young women and for
joining me on many of my writing adventures. Thank you for
helping brainstorm my stories and for assisting me at conferences.
You know I love you so very much!

Recycling programs
for this product may
not exist in your area.

ISBN-13: 978-1-335-63956-1

Five Ways to Surrender

Copyright © 2018 by Mary Jernigan

Printed in U.S.A.

www.Harlequin.com

Elle James, a *New York Times* bestselling author, started writing when her sister challenged her to write a romance novel. She has managed a full-time job and raised three wonderful children, and she and her husband even tried ranching exotic birds (ostriches, emus and rheas). Ask her, and she'll tell you what it's like to go toe-to-toe with an angry 350-pound bird! Elle loves to hear from fans at ellejames@earthlink.net or ellejames.com.

Books by Elle James

Harlequin Intrigue

Mission: Six

One Intrepid SEAL
Two Dauntless Hearts
Three Courageous Words
Four Relentless Days
Five Ways to Surrender

Ballistic Cowboys

Hot Combat
Hot Target
Hot Zone
Hot Velocity

SEAL of My Own

Navy SEAL Survival
Navy SEAL Captive
Navy SEAL to Die For
Navy SEAL Six Pack

Visit the Author Profile page at Harlequin.com.

CAST OF CHARACTERS

"Big Jake" Schuler—US Navy SEAL, demolitions expert. Big guy with a big heart he's afraid to give to any one woman. His job as a SEAL is his life.

Alexandria "Alex" Parker—Teacher living with a missionary family. She came for the adventure and to teach village children and orphans.

Abu Nuru Al-Wakesa—Leader of the Islamic State faction in Niger.

Fariji—A tall young man, eager to learn. Alex's teaching assistant at the orphanage.

Quinten Philburn—CEO of Snyder Mining Enterprises, a corporation based in the US but owned by an offshore entity.

Aaron Brightbill—US ambassador to Niger.

Thomas Whitley—Executive officer to the US ambassador to Niger.

Reverend Daniel Townsend—Elderly missionary on his last mission trip to Africa. Determined to help the poor and desperate people of Niger.

Martha Townsend—The reverend's wife of forty years. Works alongside her husband. Helps teach the women of the village life skills to grow food and keep their families healthy.

"Buck" Graham Bucker—US Navy SEAL, team medic. Went to medical school but didn't finish. Joined the Navy and became a SEAL.

"Diesel" Dalton Samuel Landon—US Navy SEAL. Gunner and team lead.

"Pitbull" Percy Taylor—US Navy SEAL. Tough guy who doesn't date much. Raised by a taciturn marine father. Lives by the rules and structure. SOC-R boat captain.

"Harm" Harmon Payne—US Navy SEAL. For a big guy, he's light on his feet and fast. Good at silent entry into buildings.

"T-Mac" Trace McGuire—US Navy SEAL, communications man, equipment expert.

Chapter One

Sweat dripped from beneath navy SEAL "Big Jake" Schuler's helmet, down his forehead and into his eyes. He raised a hand to wipe away the salty liquid, blinking to clear his vision.

Their local informant stood at the village entrance, in the Tillabéri region of Niger, talking to a barefoot man dressed in long dusty black pants and a worn button-down gray shirt. They had their heads together and appeared to be talking fast. Several times, the men glanced in the SEAL team's direction.

"What's Dubaku doing?" Jake asked into his mic.

"He's only supposed to be checking that the village is clear, before we move on," Harmon "Harm" Payne said. "You heard the brief. We're on a recon mission. We're not to engage."

Military Intelligence had gotten wind that

Abu Nuru al-Waseka, the head of the ISIS faction in north central Africa, had been seen in one of the villages farther up the road.

With what little they knew, Jake's SEAL team had deployed from their base of operations in Djibouti to Niger. From there, they hooked up with Dubaku, a member of the Niger Army who had connections with villagers along their route. Their contact had been known to help the army Special Forces unit positioned there to train the Niger armed forces. He was supposed to be a trusted source.

A prickly feeling crawled across the back of Jake's neck. "I don't like how long he's been standing there."

Dubaku turned and pointed in Jake's direction.

The man he'd been talking to nodded and re-entered the small village, disappearing around the side of a hut.

Dubaku left the village and walked along the dusty road until he reached one of the SUVs they'd commandeered from the Special Forces units. The vehicle stood partially hidden in the branches of a group of scraggly trees.

The sun baked the land, making dust out of the soil. Every puff of wind stirred the fine grains of dirt into whirling dervishes.

Using the SUV for cover, Jake hurried to Dubaku. "What did you find out?"

"The villagers haven't seen any strangers," Dubaku said.

Jake studied the man.

Dubaku didn't make eye contact. Instead, he alternated between staring at his feet and back at the village. "Ashiri went to ask others if they have seen anyone." Dubaku gave a slight bow with his hands pressed together. "If you will excuse me, I must relieve myself."

That prickly feeling multiplied when Dubaku left the SUV, walked into the sparsely wooded landscape and disappeared.

"I have a bad feeling about this," Jake said. "Let's move."

Percy "Pitbull" Taylor leaned across the cab of the SUV and flung open the passenger door. "Get in."

Jake shook his head, his gaze scanning the area and coming back to the village where Ashiri had disappeared. He gripped his rifle in his fists. "I'll walk alongside until we're past the village. I don't trust Ashiri or Dubaku at this point." Then he spoke into his mic. "Diesel, keep a safe distance between the vehicles."

"Wilco." Dalton "Diesel" Landon waited until Pitbull pulled several vehicle lengths ahead.

Graham "Buck" Buckner climbed out of Diesel's vehicle and raised his M4A1 rifle at the ready.

Harm, already on the other side of Pitbull's vehicle, moved forward as the SUV inched along at a slow, steady pace.

Buck and Trace "T-Mac" McGuire brought up the rear of Diesel's SUV. Every SEAL on the ground had an M4A1 carbine rifle with the Special Operations Peculiar Modification (SOPMOD) upgrade. Pitbull and Diesel had their weapons in the SUVs, within easy reach.

At that moment, Jake wished he had an HK MP5 submachine gun with several fully loaded clips. That prickly feeling was getting worse by the minute. Jake didn't see the normal congregation of women and children outside the huts. In fact, since they'd arrived outside the village, those people who had been hanging around had all disappeared.

"Let's move a little faster," Jake urged. "The village appears to be a ghost town."

"Something's up," Harm agreed.

"I thought this was supposed to be a routine fact-finding mission," T-Mac said.

"'Don't engage,' they said." Buck mimicked the intel officer who'd briefed them in Djibouti. "Well, what if they engage us first?"

"That's when all bets are off." Jake's hold tightened on his rifle.

The lead vehicle had passed the village and was moving along the dirt road leading to the next village when an explosion ripped through the air.

"What the hell was that?" Diesel asked.

"We've got incoming!" Harm yelled. "Someone's got an RPG and they're targeting our vehicles."

Another rocket hit the ground fifty yards from where Jake stood. He dropped to a squat and waited for the dust to clear.

When it did, he counted half a dozen men in black garb and turbans rushing toward him, firing AK-47s.

"They fired first," Jake said, returning fire. "Six Tangos incoming from the west." He took out two and kept firing.

"I count five from the east," Harm said from the other side of the SUV. Sounds of gunfire filled the air.

"Got a truckload of them coming straight at us on the road," Pitbull said.

"I count at least half a dozen comin' at us from the rear," T-Mac reported.

"We're surrounded," Buck said. "Use the SUVs for cover."

The men rolled under the SUVs and fired from beneath.

"Guys, get out from under the lead vehicle!" Pitbull yelled. "They're going to ram us!"

Jake rolled out from under and kept rolling, staying as low to the ground as he could, firing every time he came back to the prone position. He slipped into a slight depression in the hard-packed dirt and fired at the black-garbed men coming at him.

A loud bang sounded along with the screech of metal slamming into metal.

Giving only the fleetest of glances, Jake's heart plummeted. The lead SUV had been knocked several feet back from where it had been standing. If Harm hadn't made it out in time, he would have been crushed by the ramming enemy truck.

"Pitbull?" Jake held his breath, awaiting his friend's response.

"I'm good," Pitbull said. "Shaken, not stirred. I shot the truck driver before he hit."

"Good. Everyone else," Jake said, "sound off."

In quick succession, the other four men reported in.

"Harm."

"T-Mac."

"Buck."

"Diesel."

A man leaped up from the ground and ran toward Jake.

The navy SEAL fired, cutting him down, only to have another man take his place and rush his position. He pulled the trigger. At the last minute, the attacker swerved right. The bullet nicked him, but didn't slow him down.

Jake pulled the trigger again, only nothing happened. He pushed the release button, and the magazine dropped at the same time as he reached for another. Slamming the full magazine into the weapon, Jake fired point-blank as the man flung himself at Jake.

The bullet sailed right through the man's chest, and he fell on top of Jake.

For a moment, Jake was crushed by the man's weight. He couldn't move and couldn't free his hands to fire his weapon.

Gunfire blasted all around. Dust choked the air and made locating the enemy difficult at best.

Jake pushed aside the dead man and glanced around.

"They fell back," Buck said. "But they're regrouping."

"Get in the rear SUV and get the hell out of here," Jake said. "I'll cover."

Buck and T-Mac jumped into the rear SUV. Diesel revved the engine and raced up to the destroyed one.

The doors were flung open. "Get in," Buck said.

Harm ran alongside the vehicle, refusing to get inside. Pitbull pulled himself into the front passenger seat.

The enemy soldiers raced to follow them.

Jake laid down suppressive fire, emptying a thirty-round magazine in seconds.

"We're not leaving without you!" Harm yelled.

Jake shook his head and kept firing. "Get in the damned vehicle. I'll remain on the ground and cover."

Harm complied and the SUV moved forward, using the crashed SUV for cover.

Jake popped out the expended magazine and slammed in one of the last two he had.

The enemy soldiers either hit the ground when they caught a bullet, or dived low to avoid getting hit. Either way, Jake's gunfire slowed their movement. But not for long. "Go!" he yelled, lurched to his feet and backed up to the enemy truck without letting up his suppressive fire against the oncoming threat. "You have to leave now. It's the only way any of us are getting out of this alive."

Jake flung open the door of the truck, dragged the dead driver out and climbed behind the steering wheel. He hung his rifle out the window and fired with his left hand. "I'll head for the hills, head south, get to safety and come back when you have sufficient backup." He started the engine and attempted to reverse. The front grill of the truck hung on the grill of the damaged SUV.

"I don't like it," Diesel said into Jake's earpiece.

"You don't have to," Jake said. "Just go before I run out of bullets."

Diesel pulled away in the SUV.

Jake fired again, laying down a barrage of bullets at the men advancing on his position. He ducked low as bullets hit the windshield and pinged off the metal frame of the truck. He shifted into Drive, hit the accelerator and slammed the SUV. Then he shoved the shift into Reverse and gunned the engine. The SUV dragged along with him for several feet until the front grill broke free.

Jake backed up fast and considered racing after the other SUV. But, already, another truck had appeared from the direction of the village. If he didn't take out the oncoming vehicle, the rest of his team would gain little lead time on the enemy.

Shifting into Drive, Jake revved the engine and shifted his foot off the brake. The truck shot forward, plowing through the line of attackers, knocking some down and scattering the rest.

Driving head-on toward the truck, Jake held true, daring the other driver to back down first but guessing he wouldn't.

At the last moment, Jake grabbed his rifle, flung open the door and threw himself out of the truck. He hit the ground hard, tucked and somersaulted, his weapon pressed close to his chest.

The truck he'd been driving plowed into the other with the clash of metal on metal. Both vehicles shook and then settled, smoke and steam rising from the engines.

Jake didn't wait around to see what the remaining jihadist would do. He jerked a smoke grenade from his vest, pulled the ring, tossed it behind him and then ran toward the only cover he had—the short, squat mud-and-stick huts of the village clustered against a bluff. He figured the enemy wouldn't start looking for him there.

He prayed he was right. From the intel briefing they'd received, the ISIS faction was alive and well in the Tillabéri region of southwestern Niger and was known for the extreme torture tactics they used against their foes. He refused to be one of their victims. He'd die fighting rather than be captured. Surrender wasn't an option.

REVEREND TOWNSEND BURST through the door of the makeshift schoolhouse, interrupting Alex's reading lesson. "Alex, get the children out of the building. Now!"

Alexandria Parker's heart leaped into her throat. "Why? What's wrong?"

The reverend's wrinkled face was tense, his hands shaking as he waved children toward the door. "Kamathi just came through the village and told everyone to get out. If I hadn't been there, I wouldn't have known."

Alex closed her reading book. "Why do we have to leave?"

"Al-Waseka is coming."

Fear rippled through Alex. One of the men in the village had been captured by al-Waseka, the most notorious Islamic State leader in all of Niger. He had been beaten, whipped and burned in many places on his body. The only reason he'd survived was because they'd thrown his body off the back of a truck, presuming he was dead. He'd crawled under a bush and waited until his captors had left the area. Then he'd used what little energy he had remaining to wait near the road for the next friendly vehicle to pass. Fortunately, it had been the good reverend's.

In his seventies, Reverend Townsend got around well for his age. He worked hard and never complained. The villagers loved him and treated the white-haired old man and his wife like family.

Standing in Alex's makeshift schoolroom, he appeared to have aged ten years. "By the time I left the village, every man, woman and child had gone. They ran into the hills. We have to get these children out of the orphanage as quickly as possible. Take them into the hills."

Alex waved to her assistant, Fariji, the tall young man who'd been more than happy to help her with her lessons and, in the process, was learning to read himself. "Help me get the children out."

"Yes, Miss Alex." He had the older kids hold hands with the younger ones and led them out the door.

Alex herded the rest of the children toward the door. "Leave your books," she said. "Older children, help the younger ones."

The children bottlenecked at the door, where the reverend hurried them through. Once they were all outside, he faced the children. "Follow Miss Alex and Fariji," he said. "Stay with them."

Alex turned to the reverend. "Where do I go in the hills?"

"Anywhere, just hide. Some of the older children play in the hills. Let them lead you." He turned to stare into the distance, where the road led into the village.

Alex didn't like that the reverend wasn't coming with them. "What about you and Mrs. Townsend?"

"Martha refused to leave the sick baby." He looked back at her. "Go. We are in God's hands."

Maybe so, but the ISIS terrorists didn't believe in the reverend's God. They believed in killing all foreigners and many of their own people in their efforts to control the entire region. "Reverend, let me help you bring Martha out of the village."

He shook his head. "She won't abandon the

mother and child she has been helping for the past few days. They can't be moved."

"Have you considered the fact that you and your wife staying with them might give the terrorists more reason to not only kill you and your wife, but also the woman and her baby?"

He nodded and repeated, "We are in God's hands." He nodded at the children running toward the hills. "Go with them. They need someone to ensure their survival."

Torn between saving the children and saving her mentor, father figure and friend, Alex hesitated.

"You can't help everyone," the reverend said. "Martha and I have lived long, productive lives. No regrets. You and the children have not." He waved her toward the children. "Go. Live."

Alex hugged the reverend. "I'll go, but once the children are safe, I'm coming back for you and Martha."

He patted her back. "Only if it's safe."

An explosion rocked the ground and was followed by the sound of gunfire.

Her pulse hammering in her veins, Alex hurried after Fariji and the children running through the village streets toward the hills.

She counted heads, satisfied she had all

of her little charges. Some of them clustered around her, while others ran ahead. One little girl tripped and fell.

Alex scooped her up and set her on her feet, barely slowing. She clutched the child's hand and kept moving.

More gunfire sounded behind her. She didn't look back. She had one goal: to get the children to safety. Only then would she think about what was going on in the village.

At the far end of the community, they neared the base of the bluffs rising high over their heads.

A shiver of fear rippled through Alex. She had never hiked in the hills because she was afraid she wouldn't find her way back out. Now she was purposely heading into unknown territory—with children. For a moment, she hesitated.

Then another explosion shook the earth beneath her feet. She glanced over her shoulder. A plume of dusty fire and smoke rose up into the air near the road leading into the village.

She didn't need any more motivation. Bullets were bad; bombs were even worse. "Hurry!" she yelled.

The youngest children had slowed, their little legs tired from running through the village.

Alex despaired. How could she get all of them up the steep slopes? And if they did make it, where would she hide them?

She'd heard from some of the elders that there were caves in the hills. In the past, when their village had been invaded, the people had fled to the hills and hidden in the caves until the attackers moved on.

Alex lifted one of the smallest girls and settled her on her back. She started up the hill, holding the hand of a little boy, small for his seven years. She tried not to think about what was happening down in the village.

If the threat was the ISIS faction, the reverend and his wife were in grave danger. Alex's heart squeezed tightly in her chest. The elderly couple were incredibly kind and selfless. They didn't deserve to be tortured or killed.

Ahead, Alex caught glimpses of other villagers, climbing the rugged path upward. She felt better knowing they were heading in the right direction. Hopefully, the men terrorizing the village wouldn't take the time or make the effort to climb into the hills to capture villagers and orphans. What would it buy them?

However, Alex, being an American and female, might be a more attractive bargaining chip. Or she'd make for better film footage on propaganda videos. She had to keep out of sight of the ISIS terrorists.

Once they could no longer see the village, Alex breathed a little more freely. Not that they were out of danger, but if they couldn't see the village, the attackers couldn't see them.

Ahead and to the north rose stony bluffs, shadowed by the angle of the sun hitting the ridge to the south.

Alex paused to catch her breath and study the bluff. Had she seen movement? She blinked and stared again at a dark patch in the rocky edifice.

A village woman slipped from the patch and climbed downward to where Alex stood with her little band of orphaned children.

Another woman followed the first, and then another. Soon five women were on their way down the steep slope to where Alex and Fariji stood. Each gathered a small child and headed up to what Alex realized was a cave entrance.

Alex, burdened with the girl on her back, started up the path, urging the other children to climb or crawl up the slippery slope. By the time she reached the entrance, she was breathing hard.

She slipped the girl from her back and eased her to the stone floor of the cave.

More than a dozen women and children emerged from deep in the shadows, their eyes wide and wary. They gathered around Alex, all talking at once.

"Where are the others?" Alex asked in French.

"Scattered among the caves." A woman called Rashida stepped forward. "There are many caves. This is only the first one."

"They will find us here," a younger woman said. "We must go deeper into the hills."

"We can't," Rashida said. She tipped her head toward three older women sitting on the ground, their backs hunched, their eyes closed. "The old ones will not make it. It was all they could do to come this far."

Alex's heart went out to the old and young who couldn't move as fast or endure another climb up steep hills.

"None of us will last long without food and water," the other woman argued.

"We can't go back down to the village." An old woman called Mirembe glanced up from her position seated on the ground. "We would all be tortured or killed."

Alex didn't want to argue with the women when the reverend and his wife were down there with no one to help or hide them. With the children safe in the cave, Alex couldn't stop thinking about the elderly missionaries. She drew in a deep breath and made up her mind. "I need you women to care for these children."

Again, the women gathered around her.

"Where are you going?" Rashida asked.

"Don't leave us," another woman pleaded.

"If you go back, you'll be killed," Mirembe predicted.

"I have to go back. Reverend Townsend and his wife stayed behind."

Mirembe shook her head. "They are dead by now. They must be."

A sharp pain pierced Alex's heart. "I choose to think they are still alive. And I'm going down to see if there is anything I can do to help." She glanced around at the women. "Will you care for these children?" she repeated with more force.

Rashida nodded. "We will look after them until your return."

A tiny hand tugged at her pant leg. "Miss Alex, please don't go."

Alex glanced down at Kamaria, the little

girl she'd carried up the hill. She had tears in her big brown eyes as she stared up at Alex.

Her chest tight, Alex dropped to one knee and hugged Kamaria. "I'll be back," she promised. "Until I return, I need you to help take care of your brothers and sisters." She brushed a tear from the child's cheek. "Can you do that for me?"

Kamaria nodded, another tear slipping down her cheek.

Alex straightened. "I'll be back as soon as I can."

Fariji followed her to the cave entrance. "It is not safe for you to return to the village. I will go with you."

"No." Alex touched his arm. "Stay here and protect the women and children. They have no one else."

The gentle young man nodded, his brow dipping low. "I will do what I can to help."

And he always did. Fariji was one of the most loving, selfless men in the village.

Alex hugged him, and then she left the cave and slid down the gravelly slope to the base of the bluff. She figured returning to the village would be dangerous, but she couldn't abandon the missionaries. If she could help, she would, even if it meant risking her own safety.

Chapter Two

Going down from the hills alone went a lot faster than climbing, carrying a child on her back and herding half a dozen more. Within minutes, Alex reached the edge of the village.

She hid behind the first wall she came to, pushed the scarf she wore down around her neck and listened, her heart beating so loudly against her eardrums, she could barely hear anything.

The gunfire had ceased, but men shouted. A woman screamed and vehicle engines rumbled.

The reverend's wife had been in the home of a woman who'd given birth to a baby boy. The baby had been breech, complicating the birth. Both had survived, but were weak and unable to travel.

Mrs. Townsend had been caring for the two since the baby's birth.

Alex dared to peek around the side of the

hut. The narrow street between the dirt-brown mud-and-stick buildings appeared empty. She sucked in a deep breath and ran to the next structure.

A man shouted nearby. Footsteps pounded in the dirt, along with the rattle of metal against metal or plastic, like the rattle of a strap on a rifle.

Alex held her breath and waited.

Shouts grew closer. The sound of something smashing made Alex jump and nearly cry out.

She clapped a hand over her mouth and slipped farther back into the shadows.

Another man yelled, the noise coming from inside the building behind which Alex huddled.

Voices argued back and forth, and then... *bang*!

Knowing it was too late to change her mind about coming back to the village, Alex shrank into a dark corner and prayed the men in the hut didn't come out and discover her there.

The home the reverend's wife had been in was a couple huts over from where Alex hid. If she could get there without being seen, perhaps she could convince the missionaries to leave before the men found them.

Voices sounded again as the men exited the building and moved to the next.

Alex waited, fully expecting them to come around the corner and start shooting.

She froze and made herself as small as she could in the meager shadow.

A loud bang erupted nearby, as if someone had slammed a door.

The men in the street said something, and then more footsteps pounded against the dirt street, moving away from Alex's hiding place.

She let go of the breath she'd been holding. After another moment or two, she rose and eased to the corner. The street was clear.

Someone shouted from a couple houses over.

If she was going to move, she had to do it before the men returned.

Alex ran across the street, skirted another hut and checked around the next corner.

It, too, was clear.

She started across the street, heard a cry and nearly froze. Realizing she couldn't make it around the next home in time, she dived through a door and squatted inside, trying to control her breathing in order to hear the enemy's approach.

Footsteps clattered along the path outside the hut. Then they stopped.

For a long moment, Alex heard nothing. She waited a little longer and then eased toward the door.

Before she reached it, an arm wrapped around her middle and a hand clamped over her mouth, stifling a scream rising up her throat.

She struggled to free herself, but the arm holding her tightened, trapping her arms against her side and her back against a hard wall of a chest. "Shh," he whispered against her ear, his breath heated and minty. Not what Alex would have expected from an enemy rebel.

"Check in that building," someone said in French outside.

Alex froze. Though she was unsure of her captor, the men outside had been shooting. She'd make her escape from the man holding her after the other men passed in the street. Until then, she held still against the warm, hard surface of a hulking, big man with arms like steel vises. As she waited, she listened for the sound of movement outside the building.

Someone called out next to the door, "I have this one, you check the next."

The door jiggled.

The hand over her mouth dropped to her arm and she was shoved backward, behind the man.

If she wanted, she could escape him. But to what?

She couldn't go back out into the street and risk being captured by the rebels storming the village. She'd be better off taking her chances with her unknown captor in the dark interior of the hut.

The door swung inward.

Alex was shoved behind the opening door as a beam of sunlight slashed across the floor.

A man in black clothing stepped into the building, pushing the door wider with the rifle he held in his hands.

As the light beam fanned out, it chased away the darkness of the rest of the room. In the gray light out of the sunshine's wedge, Alex studied her captor.

He wore a desert-camouflage military uniform and a helmet, and carried a wicked-looking rifle of the type the Special Forces units carried. She searched for some indication of whose team he played for. Was he American, French or—God forbid—one of the paid mercenaries so often found in conflicts where they didn't belong? He wasn't from Niger. The skin she could see was too light. Granted, it appeared tanned, but not the rich darkness of the native Niger people.

The man who'd pushed open the door stepped inside the room, his weapon raised. Then he fired several bullets.

Alex flinched and shrank back into the corner. If the shooter turned any farther in their direction, he'd hit her captor.

The rebel turned slowly.

Alex's captor leaped forward, slamming the butt of his weapon into the side of the shooter's head. The weapon dropped from his hands and fell to the floor. Before the man could react, the military guy pulled a knife and slit the shooter's throat. Her captor bent to retrieve the other man's weapon. With equally efficient movements, he removed the bolt, slid it into his pocket and laid the remainder of the rifle on the ground next to the dead man.

Then her captor turned to her and held out his hand. "We have to move."

She remained frozen in her position crouched on the floor of the hut, her heart beating so fast she could barely breathe to keep up with her need for oxygen.

His hand shot out, palm up. "Now!"

Alex stared at the big, calloused hand that had just dispatched a rebel fighter with such ease and efficiency of movement. Would he do the same to her?

Shouts outside the open door of the hut shook Alex out of her stunned silence.

Her captor dropped his arm, eased up to the door and glanced out. Without turning, he spoke softly, "If you want to live, come with me now."

"Who are you?" she asked.

"Introductions later. Run now!" He hooked her arm, jerked her up off the floor and rushed her to the doorway.

After a quick pause, he dragged her out into the street and back toward the hills.

They'd gone past several huts when Alex remembered why she'd returned to the village in the first place. She dug her heels into the dirt and ripped her arm out of his grasp.

He wheeled around, his gaze shooting in all directions. "Why are you stopping?"

"I came to help Reverend Townsend and his wife," she said.

His lips pressed into a thin line. "You can't help anyone if you're dead. We have to get out of the village, before they find that man's body."

"I didn't kill him," she pointed out. "You did."

"It was him or us." The man grabbed her arm and pulled her off the street and into the shadow of one of the huts. "Now isn't the time to argue. The terrorists outnumber us twenty to one. And they won't hesitate to shoot first. If they take prisoners, they won't be kind to them."

"Exactly my point. The reverend and his wife stayed behind with a new mother and her baby. I can't leave them to the terrorists."

"You will do them no good if these ISIS bad guys capture you, as well. The best we can do is get out of here, notify someone with more firepower than we have and let them launch a rescue mission."

"Why should I go with you? I don't even know if you're one of the good guys."

"If I was one of the bad guys, I would have left you behind for ISIS to find instead of wasting my time arguing with you." He peeked around the corner of the building. "Now, if you're done flapping your jaw, we need to move."

He had an American accent, and, despite his gruff demeanor, he had saved her from being filled with bullets. Or had he saved himself? Either way, she was still alive and he was the reason.

This time he didn't grab her and drag her; he glanced back and raised his eyebrows. "Ready?"

She nodded.

He held out his hand.

Alex laid hers in his. A jolt of awareness raced up her arm into her chest. His fingers curled around hers, strong, sure and rough. A fleeting thought ran through her mind. What would it feel like to have those hands run freely over her naked body?

Shocked at her thoughts, Alex shook herself and fell in step with the man who had her life in his hands. Once he got them out of the current situation, he could do anything he wanted with her.

A trickle of fear and something else slipped down her spine. Alex refused to think past getting out of the village to somewhere safe where they could hide. For all she knew, she was trading one bad set of cards for another.

JAKE HADN'T EXPECTED to find an American woman in the village. When she'd run into the hut where he'd been hiding, he knew he couldn't leave without taking her with him.

The ISIS terrorists would either kill her, or rape and torture her until she wished she were dead. Leaving her behind wasn't an option. But taking her with him made them both more vulnerable. She slowed him down, and two people made a bigger target than just one person attempting to escape and evade capture.

With the sun starting its descent toward the horizon, their best bet would be to either make a dash for cover in the hills, or hunker down in one of the huts and wait until dark to make their move.

The crack of gunfire filled the air with the answer to Jake's question. They had to get out now rather than later. When the terrorists found the dead man, they'd be out for blood. He felt bad about leaving behind the reverend, his wife and the new mother, but he couldn't take on the entire ISIS force that had stormed the village. They were far outnumbered, and his ammo wouldn't last long enough to take out all of them.

He prayed his diversion had bought the rest of the SEAL team time enough to get away from the ISIS rebels. They would expect him to seek refuge and escape from the occupied village before attempting to reconnect with friendly forces.

Jake wondered what had happened to the drone that was supposed to be flying over while they were on their mission. Had the drone been in the vicinity of the village, they would have known the ISIS group was on its way and either been prepared for the attack or gotten the hell out of Dodge before they'd arrived.

Instead, they'd been outmaneuvered and outgunned. If Jake hadn't rammed the other truck, they would have been mowed down by the sheer number of bullets the terrorists could have unloaded into them.

Hut by hut, Jake led the way, making it to the edge of the village. He paused to assess the chances of strolling across a wide, barren expanse of land. By himself, he could low crawl or run in a zigzag line long enough to achieve the safety of cover behind some of the larger boulders at the base of the nearby hills. With the woman, he wasn't sure he could reach safety before they were discovered, and he didn't know her physical capabilities.

He ran his gaze over her length. "Can you run?"

The woman tilted her chin. "I was on the track team in high school."

"I didn't ask if you were on the track team."

He drew in a deep breath, let it out and asked again, "Can you run now?"

She frowned. A nearby shout made her jump. "Yes. Yes, I can run." She inched closer to him.

"Then on the count of three, I want you to take off in front of me and run like the hounds of hell are on your heels. Keep as low as you can. I'll be right behind you. Don't slow down until you reach those boulders at the base of the hills." He touched her arm. "Can you do it?"

Her eyes round, she pulled her bottom lip between her teeth and nodded.

After one more glance around the vicinity, Jake whispered, "Go."

For a moment, the woman didn't move. Then she took off like a bullet shot from an M4A1 rifle. He'd never seen a woman run as fast as that woman ran from the Niger village.

He almost smiled, but he didn't have time to admire her resilience and strength. He took off after her, staying as close as possible to block the bullets someone might shoot their way. He had the bulletproof vest, but the woman had nothing.

Once they were over halfway there, he began to think they'd make it without being noticed. That was not the case. The sharp report of gunfire echoed off the hillsides.

Jake automatically ducked lower, and he was glad to see the woman in front of him doing the same.

With over two hundred yards between them and the village, they could potentially make it to the hills without being shot. Hitting a still target at two hundred yards was hard enough. Hitting one that was moving was even harder. He closed the distance between himself and his lady counterpart, keeping his back between her and that village. Fifty yards. All they needed was another fifty yards, and then they could duck behind the cover of the boulders.

Something slammed into his back, pushing him forward. He stumbled and plowed into the woman, sending her flying forward. She hit the ground on her hands and knees, but kept moving, crawling as fast as she could go.

Jake regained his footing, scooped up the woman, set her on her feet and hustled her toward the boulders.

Bullets kicked up dust at their feet as they rounded a man-size rock that had fallen from the bluffs above.

After a few deep breaths to refill his lungs,

Jake stared at the woman who wasn't breathing any harder than he was. "By the way, I'm Jake."

"Alexandria Parker. Most folks call me Alex." She looked past his shoulder. "I can hear voices coming nearer. Let's go."

She stepped out with purpose, heading away from the village and up into the hills.

Jake followed. "You weren't kidding about running track."

"I run whenever I get a chance," she said without slowing to catch her breath. "Even over here in Niger."

When they came to a bend in the trail, Jake glanced back, his pulse picking up again. "Well, you're going to have to keep running. They're coming after us."

Alexandria picked up the pace, climbing higher and faster. Soon the village was completely out of view behind a hill. They couldn't keep up the pace, but, thankfully, neither could their pursuers, and they didn't have the benefit of ATVs to speed up the search.

"If you're up to it, we should keep moving until nightfall," Jake suggested.

"I'm good to go," she said, her breathing a little labored. But she didn't slow, didn't falter, just kept going.

Jake thanked his lucky stars this woman

wasn't one to fall to pieces when the going got tough. A glance ahead at the rocky path provided a good indication that the going promised to get tougher. And they had no food or water to sustain them if they had to hide out for any longer than a day or two.

At the moment, though, their number-one need was a safe haven from gunfire.

The path into the hills forked. When Alexandria turned right instead of left, he didn't question her choice. It made sense to choose the path least traveled. The other appeared to be recently disturbed.

The crack of gunfire echoed off the hillsides. As they slipped over the top of a ridge, Jake glanced back.

Several men dressed in the black garb of the ISIS rebels were climbing the path they'd taken.

"Wait on the other side," Jake commanded.

Alexandria dropped below the ridge and did as told.

Hunkering low to the ground, Jake steadied his rifle and peered through the scope, focusing on the movement below.

His hands tightened on the rifle. "Damn."

"What?" Alexandria started to climb up beside him.

Jake held out a hand to stop her and replied, "They're following our path."

"Good," Alexandria whispered. "They found the candy wrapper I left."

Anger surged as Jake sank back behind the ridge and stared at the woman as if she'd lost her mind. He stopped short of grabbing her by the arms and shaking some sense into her. "Why the hell did you do that?"

Her lips firmed and she lifted her chin. "The other path led to where the orphans and villagers are hiding in the caves. I didn't want the militants to find them."

His ire abated as he stared into the eyes of a woman who had sacrificed her own safety for that of others. He couldn't fault her for that, not when he'd done the same for his team. "Okay. I get it. But that doesn't make it any easier on us. We can't stop moving until dark." He glanced one last time over the top of the ridge.

They'd lost some of their lead. They'd have to get a move on to gain ground. He'd counted six of the ISIS fighters. The predators outnumbered the prey, but they still had the lead. With only a few rounds remaining in his magazine, Jake couldn't risk a firefight. He had to get himself and Alexandria back to his team before they were caught or died in the arid landscape.

Chapter Three

Alex's calves and thighs were past sore and now bordered on numb, but she kept climbing. Dusk settled in around her and Jake, making it more difficult to judge distance. She slipped on the path and almost tumbled down the hill they were on.

Jake grabbed her arm just in time and jerked her backward, slamming her into his broad, muscular chest.

She clung to him, appreciating his strength for a brief moment. He didn't seem to be winded at all, whereas she was breathing hard and every muscle in her body quivered with overuse. Sure, she ran and kept in good shape, but she hadn't been climbing hills, which required the use of a different set of muscles.

"We need to find shelter for the night," Jake said, his voice so close to her ear it warmed the side of her neck.

She pushed against his chest and straightened. "I can keep going." It was a lie, but she refused to be the one to hold them back. If the rebels caught up to them because of her, she would be responsible for the outcome.

"You might be able to keep going, but I'm tired and I don't have any desire to fall off a cliff in the dark."

"Okay." She stared up at the bluffs surrounding them. "These hills are riddled with caves. Will a cave suffice?"

He nodded and glanced up. "Yes."

Alex's lips twisted. "We passed several in the last valley. But, of course, when you're looking for one you can't find one."

"We'll keep moving. Maybe there will be one over the next ridge."

Jake took the lead, picking his way through the brush and bramble. The trails had become nothing more than animal paths, crisscrossing the sides of hills and seeming to have no rhyme or reason to their course. He headed toward a pass between two hills, climbing up a steep slope to reach it. He didn't linger on the ridgeline, dropping to the other side quickly to keep from being silhouetted against the fading light.

Alex did the same. When she stood beside

him on the other side of the ridge, she scanned the hillsides, cliffs and valley below.

"There." Jake pointed to several dark areas along the side of a bluff, across the narrow valley from where they stood.

Alex squinted. The dark shadows could be caves. The only way to know for certain was to get closer and check them out. With darkness settling in around them, they had to hurry or they'd be stumbling around in pitch black before the stars came out to shed a little light on their situation. And when the stars came out, that might allow for enough light that their pursuers could pick them out against the slopes and give away their hiding place before they even reached it.

Jake eased down the slippery slope one side step at a time.

Alex sucked in a deep, tired breath and hurried down the hillside, slipping and sliding on the loose gravel and stones. Her feet flew out from underneath her and she sat down hard, her momentum carrying her downward faster than she'd intended and bruising her backside as she went. She reached out, flailing for purchase, grabbing at the brush or anything that would slow her descent. The roots and brush she tried to hold on to ripped from the dry soil, barely slowing her fall.

"Watch out," she called out as her body picked up speed, heading straight for the man who'd saved her from the ISIS rebels. And she could do nothing to stop herself.

About the time Jake turned to see what was happening, she plowed into his shins, knocking him off his feet. He fell, landing on top of her.

Instead of slowing her fall, he slipped down the hillside with her, like an avalanche of human flesh, plummeting to the bottom.

When she finally came to a halt, Alex lay for a moment, trying to breathe.

Jake was still on top of her, his face dusty, his eyes wide. "Are you all right?" he asked.

She tried to say something, but she couldn't get enough air into her lungs to pass her vocal cords. "Can't..." she wheezed.

"Can't what?" he asked, untangling his legs from hers. Finally he pushed up on his arms, still leaning over her.

"Breathe," Alex said on a gasp. She filled her freed lungs with precious air. "Though we needed to get down the hill fast, I believe there could have been a better way than using me as a human sled."

He chuckled and leaned over on one arm so that he could push the hair out of her eyes. "Sorry. I couldn't move out of your way fast enough."

"No, it was my fault. I should have taken better care coming down the side of the hill."

"How bad is your backside? After sliding down a rocky hill, it's bound to be bruised and cut. Roll over, and let me take a look."

Alex shook her head. "No time. We have to make it to those caves before we're spotted by the ISIS rebels. We might make it there before them, but if they see us, we might as well be sitting ducks." Though her back hurt and she was bruised and scratched, as he'd guessed, she couldn't give in to self-pity. They had to keep moving or risk capture.

A shiver shook her frame. She'd heard what the ISIS men did to women they captured, and she didn't plan on finding out just how bad it was.

Jake rose and held out his hand.

She took it in hers, let him pull her to her feet and straightened her torn shirt.

He turned her hand over in his and studied the cuts and scratches. "You're bleeding."

Alex tugged her hand free and wiped it on her jeans. "I'll live. We need to move."

For a moment, he remained standing in front of her. Then he nodded. "We'll take care of it when we get to the cave." He hooked her arm and set off through the brush and across the narrow valley. At the valley's center was a narrow stream with running water.

Jake squatted on his haunches and scooped water into his palm. He splashed it up into his face, washing away the dust. Then he scooped another handful and drank.

Alex dropped to her knees and slipped her sore hands into the cool stream, letting the water wash away the dirt and grit from the cuts and bruises. Then she scooped some and drank, praying she didn't get deathly ill from contaminated water.

"We don't know when we'll find water again, or how long it will be until my men come back for us," Jake said. "Drink up. But make it fast."

Not willing to give their pursuers time to catch up, Alex drank as much as she could in a few precious minutes and then pushed to her feet.

Having crossed the stream, Jake held out his hand to Alex and helped her to navigate the wet stones in the shallow water, guiding her over. Her foot slipped on the last rock.

Jake pulled her into his arms and held her long enough for her to get her feet beneath her. And long enough for Alex to appreciate the warmth and solid strength of his body against her.

Heat seared a path from where their chests met all the way to her core. When he set her back from him, she ducked her head, afraid he might see the awareness in her eyes. The man had a hard body, one most women would find hard to ignore and even harder to resist.

Thankfully, Alex wasn't most women. She couldn't be so easily influenced by a man with delicious muscles and narrow hips. And the way he wore his uniform trousers, fitting snug across his tight bottom, shouldn't affect her, either. Shouldn't…but it did. Having spent the last couple hours with the man, following him through thorny brush and bramble, she should be too tired to think about how sexy this stranger was. Perhaps *because* she was tired, she was thinking naughty thoughts when she should concentrate instead on survival.

Squaring her shoulders, she picked up the pace. Darkness and distance made it harder to see that tight butt, and she didn't want to lose him. Not out in the middle of the hills in Niger. She wasn't sure what wild animals they might encounter. They weren't far from one of the major national parks and wildlife preserves. For all she knew, they'd need those last few bullets to protect them from lions or other, more dangerous animals than the humans hunting them.

JAKE KEPT MOVING, determined to find a cave to hide from the men following them. Alex would need to rest before they continued on to find a way out of the hills and away from the ISIS terrorists that had taken control of the village.

Once they'd crossed the creek, he headed up the side of a hill, following an animal path to the dark, shadowy maw on the face of a bluff. By the time they reached the cave entrance, the path was nothing more than a thin trail, probably created by some surefooted sheep, goat or deer. He'd snagged Alex's hand and held on as they navigated the treacherous hillside.

If either one of them slipped, it would be a long, bumpy way down. He wasn't sure Alex could withstand another beating courtesy of a fall. Her hands were scratched, as were her elbows. And if her torn shirt was any indication, her back would be pretty messed up, too.

Jake had wet a bandanna while at the creek and stuffed it into one of his cargo pockets on the side of his pants. When they stopped, he'd attend to her wounds. She couldn't afford to get an infection. Not when he was unsure of when his team would send out a drone to search for their whereabouts. The rescue mission could take days to find him. If the ISIS terrorists continued to hunt them, a drone might lead them straight to their location before help could arrive to extract them.

At the cave entrance Jake took out a small flashlight from his shirt pocket, aimed his weapon into the darkness and switched on the light, careful not to shine it for too long in case the ISIS predators were close enough to see the beam.

The cave didn't go back far enough for them to hide in the depths. Anyone who climbed the hill and peered inside would see the man and woman huddled against a far wall.

"Too shallow," Jake muttered.

"There's another one farther along the bluff." Alexandria motioned toward the west.

They left the shallow cave and eased along the narrow path, lit only by the stars beginning to pop out one by one in the indigo sky. Again Jake held Alexandria's hand, helping her to keep her balance.

When they reached the second cave, he

shined his light into the darkness and couldn't see the back wall. He stepped inside, his weapon pointed into the blackness.

"Aren't you afraid of animals?" Alex whispered.

"I'm more afraid of having to shoot one. If I fire a round, I give away our location."

"And if a lion comes at us?" Alex asked, her voice shaking.

"I'll do whatever it takes to keep us alive," he assured her. "Stay behind me in case something does jump out. Or better yet, wait here."

He entered the cave.

Alex followed. "If you don't mind, I'd rather face a lion than a militant."

"Suit yourself," he said, and continued his perusal of the interior of the cave.

"So, what are you? A Special Forces soldier or something like that?"

His lips quirked. "Something like that."

She stayed close enough behind him that he could almost feel the heat of her body, but not so close that she hampered his ability to use his weapon.

"Don't the Special Forces soldiers work in teams?"

"Yes."

"So?"

"So what?" He stalled, shifting the beam of his flashlight back and forth to cover every inch of the cave floor and the dark crevices that could contain wild animals. He even checked behind a large boulder near the back of the cave.

"So, where are the rest of your teammates?" she asked.

Completing his inspection, he turned to face her. "The cave is clear."

"And you haven't answered my question." She raised her brow.

"We were separated in battle." He took her hand and led her to the back of the cave and pointed to the cave floor. "You might as well bed down for the night back here. If someone does come into the cave, they won't see us immediately." He turned to leave.

She touched his arm. "Where are you going?" Her voice held a note of panic.

He covered her hand with his. "I'm going out to scout for a few minutes."

"Do you have to?" she asked, smoothing her hands over her skirt nervously.

"I like to know what other options we have if we need to beat a hasty retreat." He handed her a small penlight. "Here. Keep this. It's not much, but it will give you a little light to see by. I'll need my bigger flashlight out there."

Alex held up the flashlight that looked more like a ballpoint pen, and cocked an eyebrow. "Like that's going to do me any good against a lion."

"No, but this might." He pulled a handgun out of his belt and handed it over.

"I haven't fired a gun since my father showed me how when I was a teen." She smiled.

His lips turned upward on the corners. "I'm surprised you've fired one at all."

"Oh, my father was all about taking care of yourself." She weighed the handgun in her palm. "He wanted me to be able to defend myself. I think he wanted me to test for the concealed carry license. Only I didn't feel comfortable carrying a gun in my purse. Most of my friends only carried makeup, a credit card, driver's license and the keys to their cars. I was afraid someone would take the gun out of my purse and shoot himself accidentally. Thus, no gun in my purse."

"Do you know how to operate this, or do I need to show you?"

"I can figure it out," she said. "Especially if my life depends on it."

"Good. I'll be back shortly." He touched

her hand holding the gun. "Promise not to shoot me?"

Her lips twisted. "I promise not to shoot you."

And he left to go down into the valley and back up over the pass to see if the men who'd been following them were still on their tail.

He paused just short of the top of the ridge. Inching just to the top, he peered over to the valley below. On the valley floor, he could see the warm glow of a campfire and shadowy figures gathered around the flames.

The ISIS rebels weren't far behind them, with only a ridge standing between them.

Jake returned to the creek, rewet the bandanna and hurried back to the cave. If the cuts and scratches on Alex's back were deep, they could become infected and cause her a whole lot more grief if left untreated for any length of time.

They could stay the night, but they'd have to leave early the next morning, while it was still dark, to be gone before the terrorists made it up over the ridge.

When he arrived back at the cave, he eased into the darkness, searching for the woman who'd escaped the village with him. Nothing stirred. No sounds of breathing or indication that anyone was there.

His pulse sped as he switched on his flashlight, using the red lens setting, making it harder for anyone outside the cave to see but illuminating the interior up to three feet in front of him.

Where was she? Had he entered the wrong cave? Or had some of the rebel forces found their way around him and made off with the pretty teacher?

He drew in a shaking breath and whispered, "It's me." Then he waited, his breath lodged in his chest.

Chapter Four

As soon as Alex heard those words, she launched herself out of her hiding place behind the giant boulders and flung her arms around Jake's neck. "Thank God," she said, burying her face in the front of his bulletproof vest.

He wrapped her in his embrace and held on.

In the back of Alex's mind, she wished he didn't have on the bulletproof vest. She would like to have felt all of his body against her, imagining its warmth pressed against her cave-chilled skin.

"Hey." He set her at arm's length and chuckled. "Did you think I wouldn't come back?"

Alex shrugged, her face cast down. She didn't want him to witness the fear in her eyes when she'd come to the conclusion he wasn't coming back. "The thought did cross my mind, as I fumbled around in the pitch dark. When you came into the cave, I didn't know if you were friend or foe." She snorted. "I'd never been so happy to hear the sound of someone's voice. You were gone for what felt like forever."

He smoothed a loose strand of hair out of her face, brushing her cheek with his calloused thumb. "Sorry. I backtracked to see whether we are still being followed."

She stiffened. "And?"

He drew in a deep breath and let it out. "They're on the other side of the ridge."

Alex's heart rate sped up. "We should leave. Now."

"They've stopped for the night. I think we'll be all right for now, but we need to head out before daylight to stay ahead of them."

Her brows knit. "Are you sure? I can keep going, if you can."

He smiled. "I know you can, but we're running on empty. At the very least, we could use some sleep." He nodded toward her. "And we need to take care of your cuts and scratches before they get infected."

Alex crossed her arms over her chest. "I'm fine. I can keep going."

"I have no doubt you can, but I need the rest and I want to see your backside. You can't ignore your injuries." He spun his finger. "About-face."

She hesitated. "Really—"

"I know. You're fine. But let me be the judge. You can't see what's on your back, but I can." He twirled his finger again. "Just do it. The sooner we take care of you, the sooner we sleep."

Swallowing hard, Alex turned her back to the man who was not much more than a stranger.

He lifted the tattered remains of her shirt.

Alex held on to the front to keep it from riding up high enough to expose her breasts in the lacy white bra she wore.

When he didn't say anything for a moment, Alex's pulse quickened. "How bad is it?" Sure, it stung and burned every time her ruined shirt rubbed against her scratches and cuts.

"It's not great, but the good news is that you'll survive, as long as the wounds don't get infected." He pulled a wet cloth from his pocket and patted her back with it. The cloth had been warmed by his thigh, and his touch was gentle. One hand held her side, steadying her, while the other removed dirt and debris from her wounds. When he was done, he released the tattered ends of her shirt and let them fall back down over her body. "The shirt has to go."

Heat seared a path through her, heading south to her core. "It'll have to do for now. I don't have another."

Jake stepped back. "You can have mine."

When Alex turned to face him, a protest on her lips, she stopped, her thoughts flying out of her head as Jake unclipped the fasteners on his vest and lowered it to the ground.

Her mouth went dry and her palms filled with sweat. "What are you doing?"

He smiled. "Giving you my shirt. Granted, it might be a little sweaty, but it will be better than what you have on."

He unbuttoned his uniform jacket and slipped out of it. Then he yanked his T-shirt up over his head in one fluid, ever-so-sexy move.

He stood in front of her wearing only his trousers and boots, his broad chest shining in the dim glow of the red-lensed flashlight. The man looked like a Roman gladiator, all hard muscles, strength and magnetism.

Alex lost her ability to form thoughts and words. Her gaze swept over the massive amount of skin stretched tautly over his frame.

When he handed her his T-shirt, she gulped. Her fingers touched his and a shock of fire raced through her hand and up her arm. "Thank—" she squeaked, cleared her throat and tried again. "Thank you."

The man turned his back to her, allowing her the privacy to shed her shredded shirt and slip the T-shirt over her head. It smelled of male, that outdoorsy scent that made her insides quiver. The fabric slid over her breasts and torso and hung down to her knees.

"I'm decent," she said. "Thanks again."

He turned, a smile spreading across his face. "It's a little big."

"But better than nothing." She wadded the torn shirt into her fist.

"Let me have that." He reached out for the ruined shirt.

Again her hand touched his. This time he glanced up sharply, as if he too felt the electric shock. Just as quickly, he looked back down at the fabric in his grip. "I want to bind the wounds on your hands."

"They'll be okay," she said.

"You need some protection to prevent further injury to your palms if you slide down another hill." He ripped a piece off the front of her shirt. Then he took her hand and wrapped it gently over the cuts and scratches, tucking the end in to keep it from unraveling.

The whole time he held her fingers in his, she couldn't breathe; nor could she control her wildly racing pulse.

When he had finished both hands, he released her and stepped back. "We need to get some rest. Morning will come all too soon."

"Shouldn't we stand watch?" she asked.

"Actually, I'd planned on staying awake and keeping an eye out for trouble."

"You need rest as much as I do." Alex lifted her chin. "I can take the first shift."

"I don't mind staying awake all night. I'm used to it. It's part of the job."

"I can stay awake half the night," Alex insisted. "I'd rather you get some sleep to keep sharp."

He studied her for a moment. "Keep an eye on the valley below. If you see any movement whatsoever, wake me immediately. Even if it's an animal scurrying out from under a rock. Wake me." His brows drew downward. "Understand?"

She popped a salute and smiled. "Yes, sir." Then she took up a position at the mouth of the cave and sat, leaning her back against the stone wall.

A glance at Jake proved he was taking her up on her offer to get some sleep. He lay on the hard floor of the cave, bunched her shirt beneath his head and crossed his arms over his chest. "Do you need the light?" he asked.

"No," she said. "The stars are enough light for me to see by."

There was a soft click, and the red glow from the flashlight blinked out.

Alex could just barely discern the outline of the man lying on the ground, but she didn't need to see him to know he'd be there for her if she needed him. The least she could do was let him sleep while she kept watch.

Staring out into the night, she scanned the valley below again and again, going over all that had happened leading up to their escape. Some things still niggled at her.

"Are you army Special Forces or something else?"

"Something else," he replied.

"Delta Force?" she guessed.

He snorted. "Please."

Not army Special Forces or Delta Force...

"Mercenary?" she tried again.

"I don't get paid enough to be a mercenary," he replied.

"What does that leave?" She glanced over her shoulder. "Marine?"

"Navy," he replied.

"Don't you need a ship nearby to be in the navy? Or at least a body of water?"

He chuckled. "Not if you're a navy SEAL."

"You're a navy SEAL?" she asked, unable to keep the awe from her voice. "Aren't they the best of the best?"

"So we're told."

She glanced back at him. "What were you doing in the village?"

"Intel had it that ISIS was in the vicinity," he said. "We were on a recon mission."

"Recon?"

"We were only out seeking further intelligence. We weren't there to engage."

"But you did," she pointed out.

"Only because they surprised us. We thought they'd be several miles up the road. We were supposed to have some drone support."

"I take it you didn't get it?"

"No." His voice was hard.

"Did the rest of your team make it out?" she asked softly.

"I hope so." For a long moment, silence reigned in the cave.

"What brought you to Niger?" he asked.

Alex stared out at the night, thinking back

over her reasons for leaving Virginia and her home. "I needed a new start, and I wanted to go somewhere I could make a difference with my teaching and my ability to speak French."

"Sounds like a breakup," Jake said.

She shrugged, though he wouldn't see the movement. "Yeah. It was something like that." She had broken up with her fiancé, realizing he wasn't the right man for her. They'd been together since their first year in college. He'd proposed after they'd been together for six years.

When they'd started planning the wedding, something had made her step back and rethink her decision to marry Paul. He'd been a good friend, and she liked his company, but there wasn't any spark and no fire in their kisses. Sex with Paul had been something she did because she knew it was expected, not because she couldn't wait to get naked and in bed with him.

Rather than go into the sad details of her less-than-exciting life, she asked, "What about you? Are you married? Do you have kids, a dog and the house with the white picket fence back in the States?"

He didn't answer for a while.

"You don't have to answer," Alex said. "It's none of my business."

"You're right," he said. "It's none of your business."

A flare of anger surged inside Alex, but she bit her tongue and refused to rise to his tart retort.

"I figured the life of a navy SEAL wasn't conducive to marriage or long-term relationships. So, no. No wife, no kids, no dog or white picket fence. Just me and my team. I keep it simple."

Alex told herself to leave the conversation there. But she couldn't help asking, "Did you ever want more?"

Again the silence stretched between them.

"Sorry, I shouldn't ask such personal questions," she whispered.

"The answer to your question is yes. There was a time when I was fairly new to the team that I thought I wanted it all. I thought I could have it all." He sighed. "I was wrong."

"I'm sorry," Alex said.

"For what?"

Her heart pinched. "That things didn't work out for you."

"I'm not. The relationship wasn't meant to be. Once a SEAL, always a SEAL. It takes a special person to put up with our lifestyle. I don't believe she exists for me. Now, let me sleep."

"Right. Zipping my lips here." She clamped her mouth shut and refused to ask a hundred more questions of the navy SEAL. He needed sleep, and it truly wasn't any of her business that he didn't think there was a woman who could love him and the life he'd chosen to lead.

Deep in Alex's heart, she knew the man was wrong. But who was she to tell him that there was someone for everyone when she hadn't been completely convinced herself?

JAKE LAY FOR a long time with his eyes closed, willing himself to sleep. Normally he didn't have a problem dropping off into light sleep when he knew he needed the mental and physical recharge only rest could provide.

But sleep wasn't coming, and the more he lay there, the more he realized it was because of the woman sitting by the mouth of the cave. Since finding her in the village, he'd had a difficult time focusing on the mission at hand.

Alex's silky black hair, hanging down to her waist in straight lengths, made Jake want to reach out and run his fingers through the strands. And those ice-blue eyes made him

look twice. He could swear he saw the vast-
ness of the universe reflected in their depths.
And her alabaster skin fairly glowed in the
darkness.

She was beautiful, smart and physically
capable of keeping up with the grueling trek
through the hills and rocky terrain. She hadn't
complained, even after sliding down the side
of a hill, scraping the skin off her hands and
backside. She was one tough lady, and she
stirred up more feelings inside Jake than he
cared to acknowledge.

The last time he'd felt this way he'd been
too eager to make a relationship permanent,
only to discover the woman he had fallen for
wasn't willing to wait for him to return home
from deployments.

Trish had left him after his very first deploy-
ment. While he'd been gone, dreaming about
her, she'd found a civil service employee on
the navy base who would be home each night
to see to her every want and need. With him,
she would never have to worry that he'd return
from work in a body bag or be deployed nine
months out of the year to some godforsaken
place he couldn't even discuss.

That was when Jake had sworn off meaning-
ful relationships that lasted more than a date or

two. He didn't have time for the games, and he didn't need the heartache. His team depended on him to have a level head and solid focus.

He opened his eyes and stared at the silhouette of the woman he'd rescued from the village overtaken by the ISIS terrorists. She wasn't someone who took the easy way out. She'd come to Africa to start over. And, boy, had she. Teaching orphans in a poor village had to be completely different from her life in the States, yet she'd done it. Not only had she taught them, she'd gotten her orphans out of the village when the terrorists stormed the streets. And she'd returned to help her missionary sponsors.

How many women had he known who would fearlessly head back into danger to help someone else?

Alex had gumption. She was the kind of woman who wouldn't settle for *safe* and *boring* in a relationship. But was she the kind of woman who could stand long separations from her significant other? What had been the reason for her breakup?

Jake found himself wanting to know more about Alex. But he needed to sleep so that he could be refreshed enough to continue the trek out of the hills and back to some measure of safety, away from the terrorists.

Thinking about Alex was pointless. Once he got her out of this situation, he probably wouldn't see her again. Why waste his time mooning over a beautiful woman? Hadn't he proved he wasn't cut out for anything more than a quick fling?

Alex didn't strike him as a quick-fling kind of woman.

With a sigh, he closed his eyes and willed himself to sleep. And he must have drifted off, because he woke with a start after what felt like only a few minutes.

"Jake," a soft, feminine voice called out to him.

He sat bolt upright, his gaze going to Alex. "What's wrong?"

"Nothing, but I'm nodding off. I can't keep watch through my eyelids." She wrapped her arms around herself and yawned. "And it's getting cold out here."

He glanced at his watch. "Four hours to sunrise. You should have woken me an hour ago."

"You were sleeping so peacefully I hated to disturb you."

He rose and crossed to where she sat with her back against the wall of the mouth of the cave.

Alex shivered and yawned at the same time. "I can't quit yawning," she said into her hand.

"Then lie down and catch some z's. I'll keep watch."

She didn't move. "If it's all the same to you, I'll just nap here, sitting up. I'm betting the floor of the cave is as cold and hard as it looks."

He nodded and stretched the kinks out of his back before sitting beside her. "It is." He held open his arms. "I can offer you an alternative if you don't mind snuggling with a stranger."

"Right now—" she yawned again and laughed "—I'd snuggle with a bear just to get warm."

"I'm not a bear, but it might help to share body warmth." He slipped his hand behind her back and pulled her against his side. "I promise not to bite."

Her belly rumbled. "I make no such promises. And I'd appreciate it if you didn't mention biting, eating or food. I'd give my right kidney for a hamburger about now."

He wrapped his arms around her and held her close against his body. "Better?"

She was stiff at first, pressed against him but not letting her body relax.

He leaned back and stared down at the top of

her head. "We haven't known each other long, but I'm not in the habit of taking advantage of women when I'm trying to escape and evade hostile enemy forces."

She tipped her head to stare into his eyes. "Did I say I was afraid of you?"

"No, but you won't get any sleep unless you relax."

"You're right." With a heavy sigh, she burrowed into him and rested her cheek against his chest. "Thank you for rescuing me from the village."

"You're welcome. Now hush and sleep."

"Yes, sir," she said smartly, the effect ruined by a huge yawn. "I am warmer. Didn't know they had bears in Niger," she mumbled.

"I didn't know they had beautiful black-haired, blue-eyed women in Niger," he whispered into her hair.

Her body relaxed against his, and her breathing became more regular and deep.

Alex slept, nestled in his arms.

Jake remained vigilant, afraid that if he fell asleep he wouldn't wake soon enough to get them out of the valley and over the next hill before the enemy found them.

The night stretched, long and cool. With Alex's body resting against his, he managed to stay warm enough.

She shivered several times, and, each time, he tightened his hold, trying to cover as much of her as he could with his arms.

His stomach rumbled, protesting the lack of food. They'd run short on energy as their bodies burned up the last of their fuel.

Jake knew he had to get them back on the road as soon as possible for his team to have even a ghost of a chance of finding them. And he needed to do it before he did something stupid, like fall for this courageous, beautiful woman.

Chapter Five

Just before dawn, Alex was nudged awake by a hand smoothing over her soft hair and a voice that whispered, "Time to go, sweetheart."

She cracked an eyelid and stared up at the man leaning over her. Had she imagined the endearment? "Are we leaving?" she asked, blinking open both eyes.

What a wonderful face to wake up to, and what a sturdy body to hold her through the night. She didn't want to wake and face the reality of their situation, not when she was wrapped in warm arms and feeling so incredibly safe.

"We are," he said. "The sun will be up within the next hour. We have to be over the next ridge before that happens."

Alex sat up and rubbed the sleep from her eyes. "But it's still dark out."

"True, but we don't want to wait until light.

If we can see better, so can the enemy. We have to get out of this area before they enter it."

"I know, but I was having the best dream about eating eggs, bacon and hash browns. Could I go back to sleep long enough to finish my meal?"

"Sorry, but it's time to rise and shine." He rose to his feet, stretched and then held out a hand to her.

She grasped his hand in hers and let him pull her to an upright position. Stiff from all the climbing she'd done the day before, she stumbled and fell against Jake's broad chest.

The SEAL held Alex close until she could get her feet firmly beneath her. She couldn't tell him that part of her problem was how giddy and unsteady she felt around the handsome man. He'd likely laugh her all the way back to his buddies.

Then again, he'd been so kind and gentle the previous day, tending her wounds and holding her through the night. For such a big, rugged man, he was sweet and patient with her. Or was he just trying to keep her healthy so that she wouldn't slow them down on their mission to survive?

She straightened her shoulders and faced the task ahead. "Let's do this."

"Are you sure you're steady enough on your feet to make it down the slope?"

"You mean without sliding on my butt to the bottom?" Alex snorted. "I promise to be a little more graceful, if at all possible. I don't relish a repeat performance of yesterday." She held up her hands, which were still neatly bandaged with the remnants of her blouse. "I can't afford to tear any more clothing. All I have is what I'm wearing. I'd like to make it to civilization with at least your T-shirt on my back."

"That's the spirit. I'll go first. That way, if you fall, you'll bump into me."

"And I'll take you with me, as I slide all the way down." She shook her head. "You'd do better staying far away. We can't afford for both of us to be injured."

"Nevertheless, I'm going first." He stepped over the lip of the cave's mouth and started down the hill. The gray light of dawn had only just begun to lighten the sky from pitch black to a dark battleship gray.

Jake picked his way down the hill, holding his hand out to steady Alex's descent while looking over the valley to make certain they weren't spotted or being followed.

She could have gotten down the slope on her own, but she appreciated that his strong hand provided stability and showed his concern for her safety. He probably only cared that she didn't break something and make his job of getting them out of there alive a lot harder.

Alex did her part and carefully placed every footstep. She refused to slide down another hill and risk taking Jake with her.

Once at the base of the hill, Jake snapped a branch off a leafy tree and handed it to her. "Drag this behind you to cover our tracks."

She did, careful to make sure the leaves stirred the prints left in the dust without looking like someone had dragged a branch over them.

Jake led her along the stream, urging her to keep to the shadows as much as possible. Every so often, she checked over her shoulder, expecting to see the ISIS fighters close on their heels. Thankfully, they weren't.

By the time the sun rose high enough to light the sky, Alex and Jake had reached the top of another ridge. Jake hurried her over the edge and paused long enough to check through his rifle scope.

Alex leaned close without raising her head above the ridgeline. "Do you see them?"

"Not yet." He shifted his concentration from the scope to viewing the entire valley with his naked eye. He stiffened. "No, wait. They just popped up over the other side of the valley." He watched a little longer. "One, two, three, four, five, six."

Jake ducked down beside her. "They don't seem to want to give up."

"What can we do?"

His jaw tightened. "Keep moving." He helped her to her feet and led the way through the hills, telling her they were heading south-west toward the city and hopefully they'd find a road that wasn't overrun by ISIS militants.

After two hours hiking in the hills, they found a dirt road and followed it for another mile. It wound around the side of a bluff and dipped down into a valley. When they came out of the vegetation to the other side of yet another hill, Alex gasped.

Jake snagged her arm and pulled her back into the brush. From there, they peered through the branches and observed the bustle of activity before them.

Where a hillside had once been now lay a giant, gaping hole with terraces spiraling down into a pit. People swarmed the pit, half-dressed, barefoot and covered in dirt. They carried buckets of mud on their heads or in their arms, or dragged them behind them as they climbed out of the pit like ants.

A backhoe dug deeper at the bottom of the pit, shoveling giant scoops of dirt into the backs of dump trucks. When the trucks were full, they rumbled up the narrow terraces to the top and emptied their contents in a huge pile.

"What's going on?" Alex asked.

"It appears to be a mining operation."

Alex frowned. "I didn't know there was one this close to the village. Most of the villagers would have known about any potential for jobs in the area."

"We've covered a considerable amount of ground since we left the village."

"Yes, but the villagers would have moved for the opportunity to work at a paying job. Those are hard to come by in rural Niger." She nodded toward a man standing on the edge of the pit, carrying a rifle and dressed like the ISIS militants. "Do you see what I see?" she whispered.

He nodded, pulled a camera out of his pocket and snapped several pictures.

"Why the pictures?"

"When we get back to civilization, I want to show the intel folks what we found." He tucked the camera back into his pocket and stood. "I don't think we want to announce our presence to these guys. Come on. We can move around the periphery and get the hell out of here."

Alex followed Jake on a circuitous route skirting the mining operation, giving it a wide berth.

As they neared the opposite end of the mine and nearby camp, Jake paused to snap more pictures, including some of the trucks hauling dirt out of the pit. They had some kind of logo on them.

"Look out," Jake whispered. "Our guys are entering the camp." He nodded toward the road where they'd been standing less than thirty minutes prior.

Six men dressed in black, their heads swathed in turbans, emerged from the brush and walked straight into the mining camp.

"That's our cue to leave," Jake said. He took Alex's hand and led her into the brush, following a course that paralleled the road leading into the camp. They stayed far enough away from the road to keep out of sight, but close enough that they wouldn't lose their way.

When they had gone a mile from the camp, Jake came to a halt and tilted his head to listen. "There's a truck coming." He glanced at

Alex. "Stay here. I want to get a closer look at one of those vehicles."

Alex touched a hand to his arm. "But someone might see you."

"I'm good at blending into my surroundings. But I need to know you'll stay put and hide until I come back for you."

She chewed her lip, not liking that he was going to leave her to go near the road and risk the possibility of being captured. If he was, Alex wasn't at all sure what she was supposed to do.

He held up his hand. "I promise not to do anything dumb."

"Good. Because I don't want to have to fight my way into that camp to free you."

He chuckled. "You won't have to. I'm not going to get caught."

"Yeah," Alex muttered. "Famous last words."

He was going no matter what she said, so she kept her mouth shut, found a cluster of bushes and hid behind them. Through the leaves, she watched as Jake moved from the shadow of one tree to another. Before long, he disappeared, the shadows and leaves blending with his camouflage uniform.

A fly buzzed around Alex's head, and she was certain one was climbing up her leg, but she didn't dare move. Call her superstitious, but she was afraid if she took her gaze off the path Jake had taken, even for a second, he'd be lost to her.

Her heart hammering against her ribs, Alex lay in the bushes, counting the minutes until Jake's return. She prayed he'd come back for her. If he didn't, she would just have to go find him and bring him back herself.

JAKE CUT THROUGH the brush, angling toward the dirt road leading into and out of the copse of trees that had been their temporary sanctuary. He prayed Alex would stay hidden while he nosed around.

The rumble of a truck's engine alerted him to a vehicle approaching on the road.

Jake eased forward and dropped down behind a bush, getting as low to the ground as he could. He pulled the camera out of his pocket, aimed it at the road and waited for the truck to pass.

A modified SUV rolled by first. The top had been removed and a machine gun mounted in the center. A black-garbed soldier manned the weapon, turning left and right as they traversed the dirt road. The SUV kicked up dust behind it, temporarily clouding Jake's vision and the viewfinder of the camera.

A few moments later, a large truck came into view. The body of the truck was white, with a company logo painted in red lettering on the side.

He snapped a picture of the logo as the truck passed.

Snyder Mining Enterprises.

Another vehicle brought up the rear. This one was a pickup with another machine gun mounted in the bed and another black-garbed fighter perched behind the weapon, holding on as the truck bumped over the uneven surface.

As the vehicle neared Jake's position, the gunman in the rear banged a hand on the roof of the truck. The driver slowed to a stop.

Jake held his breath and sank lower into the brush and dirt.

The man in the back said something to those in the truck. Another man similarly dressed dropped down out of the passenger seat and climbed into the bed of the truck while the original gunman jumped out.

He walked toward the bushes where Jake lay hidden.

Jake braced himself for attack, slipped his knife from the scabbard on his ankle and waited for the man to get close enough to see him.

The ISIS gunman stopped short of the bush, lifted his shirt, unbuttoned his pants and relieved himself not two feet from where Jake lay.

Jake didn't move a single muscle, praying the man would move on as soon as he was finished.

Instead, he adjusted his clothing, frowned and stepped another foot closer to the bush.

A man shouted from the truck.

The gunman leaned close to the bush.

Jake gripped his knife, willing his heartbeat to a slow, steady pace, and prepared to launch himself at the soldier.

Another yell from the man in the truck caused the one on the ground to spin and jog back to the vehicle. He climbed into the passenger seat and closed the door, and the truck jerked forward and sped after the others.

Jake lay for a moment, until the vehicles were completely out of sight. Then he crawled backward several yards before he dared to straighten and run back to find Alex.

When he reached the copse of trees and brush, he whispered, "Alex?" and held his breath.

"I'm here," she said, and climbed out into

the open. "I heard the sound of engines. I was afraid they'd found you."

He shook his head. "They were close, but they didn't see me. Now that they're gone, we can continue to follow the road. Not on it, but parallel. Are you up for more hiking?"

She nodded. "I'm hungry, but still able to march."

"Do you want me to sneak into the camp and steal some food?"

She shook her head, her eyes wide. "No way. The people working in that mine need it more than we do."

"Agreed. Let's find our way back to my men. I'm sure they have a packet of MREs you're going to love."

"Meals ready to eat?" Alex smiled. "We get those at the orphanage sometimes. They beat starving any day."

Again Jake took the lead, with Alex following close behind. They traveled several miles just out of view of the road.

Eventually, they came to a point where the road ended in a T-junction.

"Which way?" Alex asked.

"West," he said, and turned right. "We came in from the west. If the guys made it back to camp, they will be returning this way to find me soon. In the meantime, we need to get as far away from the mine as possible."

"Agreed." Alex shivered. "I have no desire to come face-to-face with the barrel of a rifle."

They continued along the road, walking and resting intermittently until the sun dipped low in the sky, heading for the horizon.

Night two settled in around them. This time, they didn't have the relative safety of a cave to hide in. They'd moved out of the hills onto the plains, broken up by stumpy trees and bushes. Occasionally, elephants trumpeted in the distance, and they would spot a herd of African buffalo or a couple of giraffes plucking leaves out of a tree. At one point, they spotted a pride of lions lazing in the sun.

Jake kept them moving, staying as far away from the lions as he could without getting too close to the road.

Whenever a vehicle lumbered down the road, he and Alex hunkered behind a bush until it passed.

With dusk settling in, Jake worried they wouldn't be safe sleeping on the ground. After passing the lions, he was determined to find a better alternative. Alas, they didn't have many choices, and Alex's energy reserve was fading fast.

Finally they came upon a village along the road. From a perch on a small rise in the terrain, Jake and Alex studied the layout.

Just outside the walls of the village was a well. Women and children gathered around, filling buckets and jugs.

Alex licked her lips. "I could use a drink of water," she whispered.

"Me, too. We have to stop for the night somewhere."

She frowned. "Are we stopping here? Is it safe?"

"No. But we can wait until dark and sneak over to the well, drink and then leave."

Alex nodded. "I like the idea. But is it safe?"

"I haven't seen a single ISIS militant since we stopped here."

"That doesn't mean they aren't hiding out behind the walls," Alex pointed out.

"True. But if we play our cards right, we can get that drink in the dark and be gone before they have any idea we're here."

Alex nodded. "I really would like a drink. And a hamburger. But I'll settle for water."

"Then water it is." Jake glanced at the sky. "We probably have an hour until dark. I don't think anyone will climb up here and find us, so we might as well rest."

"Good. We didn't get much sleep last night."
Alex stretched, lay back on the ground, closed
her eyes and laced her hands behind her neck.

Jake smiled down at the woman. She had to
be hurting. No matter how much she worked
out, the pace they'd kept through the hills had
been grueling. Even *his* muscles were sore.

He looked down at the village once again.
With no sign of ISIS militants and only women
and children moving about, he decided he
could afford to at least rest, if not sleep. He'd
have to stay awake and keep vigilant. One
truck full of ISIS soldiers could ruin everyone's day.

Still, he couldn't resist lying beside Alex.
Dusty from a day and a half traveling cross-
country on foot, she was still the most beautiful woman he'd seen in a long time, with
curves in all the right places and a smile that
made his knees weak every time she turned it
in his direction.

"When we get back to my team, we can contact the American embassy in the capital city
of Niamey," Jake said. "I'm sure they can help
you get to the States safely."

She raised an eyebrow in challenge. "Who
said I was going to the States?"

He turned on his side and propped himself

up on his elbow. "I'd think that after what happened in that village, you'd want to go home."

"I don't want to go to the States. I have no one waiting for me there. Why would I want to go back?"

"You can't seriously consider returning to the village?"

She shook her head. "Only to help Reverend Townsend and his wife." Alex chewed on her bottom lip. "I hope they're okay."

"I'll check with headquarters when we rendezvous with my team. Maybe they'll authorize an extraction mission to free the reverend and his wife."

"That would be wonderful," Alex said.

"No guarantees, though," Jake amended.

Alex opened her eyes and stared up into his. "Don't you think they'll authorize a mission to free fellow Americans?"

If it were up to him, he'd conduct the mission himself. But he wasn't calling the shots. "I'll see what we can do. That's all I can promise." There might be even more dangerous and important missions than saving two missionaries from being overtaken by ISIS rebels. But he didn't say that to Alex. As far as she was concerned, the reverend and his wife were the number-one priority in her world. He couldn't blame her. He'd do his best to convince his commander that they needed to conduct the extraction as soon as possible. Which made it even more imperative for them to find their way back to his team.

The sooner he reunited with his teammates, the better chance they had of finding the missionaries alive. The longer it took to launch a rescue mission, the less chance they had of living through their captivity.

First, though, they had to get water in order to continue their journey. And they had to do it without being detected.

Chapter Six

"Alex, wake up." Jake's voice seemed to come to her in a dream.

Alex must have fallen asleep. When she opened her eyes, she thought for a moment she hadn't actually lifted her eyelids, it was so dark. Then she turned her head and saw a star twinkling in the heavens and realized it was night. She sat up straight and pushed her hair out of her face. "How long have I been asleep?" she asked.

"A couple of hours. It appears as if the people of the village have all gone to sleep. If we want to get water, now is the time to do it."

"I'm ready." She rolled to her feet, every muscle in her body reminding her that she'd abused it. She took a moment to stretch and turn, working out the stiffness.

Jake stood beside her, staring down at the village below and the well out in the open.

"I think it would be best if you stayed here. I can fill my helmet and bring it back to you to drink."

She shook her head before he finished. "I'm going with you. You need someone watching your back. You'll be out in the open."

"I can manage. I don't want you exposed to some sniper's scope."

Alex tilted her head to the side and stared at Jake in the light from the stars. Damn, he was handsome when he was worrying about her safety. "Have you seen any evidence that this village is occupied by snipers?"

"I've seen young men," he said. "None of them were armed."

"Have you seen any of the ISIS rebels?"

He shook his head. "Not yet."

"Not yet isn't good enough." She lifted her chin, prepared to argue. "I'm going with you."

His lips quirked. "Are you always so determined?"

She nodded once, firmly. "I am, when I'm right."

"So be it." He started down the hill toward the village, circled the huts and paused beneath a tree.

Alex trailed behind and then stepped up beside Jake. Together they studied the open area around the well. As soon as they left the shadow of the tree, they'd be in the open, visible to anyone watching.

After five minutes, Jake drew in a deep breath and let it out slowly. "Well, let's do this."

"We're just a couple of travelers looking for a drink of water," Alex whispered, her mouth dry, parched. At that moment, she'd brave the ISIS terrorists for a single cup of water. She hooked her arm through Jake's.

"Just a couple of travelers, huh?" he chuckled. "One with a rifle and a bulletproof vest. Right." He shook his head and lowered his weapon to hang beside his leg, hopefully hiding it from the casual observer.

They stepped into the open, strolled to the well, found a bucket on a rope and lowered it until it splashed in the water below.

Moments later, Jake had pulled up the bucket, filled with cool, clean water.

Alex practically fell into it, pouring it into her mouth, the refreshing liquid spilling over her chin and down the front of the borrowed T-shirt. Once she'd had her fill, she waited while Jake had his.

When he had slaked his thirst, he glanced around. "We should go."

The sound of footsteps rushing toward them made Alex spin to face the oncoming threat.

A woman with a shawl draped over her hair rushed out of one of the huts and ran straight for where Alex and Jake stood. She motioned for them to follow. "Hurry," she insisted.

"But where are we going?" Alex asked.

"Does it matter?" she asked in perfect English. "You must hide. Now."

"We don't want to bring danger to you or your people," Alex insisted. "We can hide in the trees."

"No, you don't have time." She took Jake's hand. "Come."

Jake shot a glance toward Alex. "Stay close."

She nodded, and three of them ran toward the mud-and-stick huts.

An older man held open the door as the woman led them through the outer walls into a narrow alley between huts. She navigated the twists and turns so quickly Alex was afraid they'd lose her.

But the woman had a tight hold on Jake's hand and refused to release him until they were somewhere she deemed safe. Through the maze of streets and alleys, they were led deeper into the village.

Alex was amazed at all the homes they

passed as they moved farther away from the well and the road.

Behind her, the sound of vehicle engines roared into the village common area.

Alex picked up the pace, keeping close to Jake and the woman. Gunfire echoed off the hills, making her duck. More shots were fired, filling the night with a sense of terror.

Just when Alex thought they would never stop, their guide paused in front of a structure. "In here." She flung open the door and waved them inside.

Alex entered, appalled at how small the interior room was. How would they be hidden if ISIS searched each home one by one?

The woman entered behind them and then squeezed around Jake. She bent, swept aside a rug and pulled up a mat that hid a wooden door in the floor of the hut. She opened it and waved frantically. "Get in. They will be here soon."

Alex glanced down at a dirt cellar in the floor of the primitive hut.

"We need to get in. If the ISIS militants find us here, they will punish anyone who helped to hide us." Jake dropped down into what was nothing more than a hole in the ground. He held up his arms. "Now you."

Alex didn't like the idea of being in a small

hole in the ground that could be plagued with spiders or snakes. A shiver rippled down her spine, but what choice did she have?

Shouts sounded outside.

Alex sat on the edge of the hole in the floor.

Jake reached up, grabbed her around the waist, and pulled her into the darkness and into his arms.

The woman closed the wooden trapdoor. The sound of the mat and the rug being slid into place was reassuring at the same time as it was frightening. What if the woman had tricked them into giving up their freedom? What if she had led them into her cellar to imprison them?

Alex's chest knotted. She stood in the cramped space, wrapped in the warmth of Jake's arms, counting the passing minutes, praying whoever was shaking up the village wouldn't continue their own brand of terror. She prayed for the woman who'd shared her home and hiding place to protect them from being captured and potentially tortured or killed by the militants.

Gunfire erupted outside the little hut.

Alex tensed, her fingers digging into the fabric of Jake's uniform jacket.

His arms tightened around her. "It'll be

okay," he whispered into her ear, his warm breath making her heart beat faster for an entirely different reason. She couldn't get closer to him while he wore the bulletproof vest, but his arms around her were all him, all muscle, and made her feel protected, shielded from danger.

He'd already rescued her from one situation. Between the two of them and the generosity of the village woman, they'd get out of this one, as well.

Loud voices sounded outside the hut. The door slammed open, reverberating through the small building.

Alex kept perfectly still, her ears perked for sounds.

The woman who'd hidden them spoke softly to someone.

An angry male voice yelled, "Get out!"

The shuffle of footsteps was followed by heavier steps. Something crashed above, as if a box or chair had been overturned. Another crashing sound, and then a loud bang of a shot fired at close range.

Alex clung tighter to Jake, fully expecting the next round to pierce the wooden door over their heads. She tried to shield Jake's body with her own. If the gunman fired into the cellar, he'd get her first. And maybe the bullet would be slowed enough not to enter Jake, as well.

Those thoughts raced through Alex's head as the man above stomped through the small hut, destroying the woman's meager belongings. Then he stepped out, yelling to someone else outside.

Afraid to let go of the breath she'd been holding, Alex waited, listening.

After several long minutes, the voices grew faint and the gunfire ceased. The roar of vehicle engines sounded in the distance.

"Do you think they're gone?" Alex asked, her voice so soft she doubted even Jake could hear it.

"I think so, but we should remain here a little longer to be sure." He still held her in his arms, and she didn't fight to be free.

Jake raised a hand and cupped her face in the darkness. "Are you all right?"

She nodded. "Just a little scared."

He laughed softly. "Me, too."

A few minutes later, the sound of a grass mat sliding across wood was followed by the trapdoor being pulled up. The woman who'd hidden them stood on the dirt floor above, her face a blur in the dark. "They are gone. You can come out."

"You first," Jake said to Alex. He gripped her around her waist, but before he lifted her, he bent his head and brushed her lips with his. "You were brave."

Too shocked by the kiss, Alex didn't have time to respond before she was lifted to where she could sit on the side of the hole. She swung her legs around and pushed to her feet.

Jake handed her his rifle, and then dragged himself out of the hole to stand beside them in the dim glow from the stars shining through the open door of the hut. Even the little bit of light was better than the darkness of the tiny cellar.

Jake glanced around the single room. Every box, basket or container had been dumped over, the contents spilled onto the dirt. The pallet of rags in the corner that was probably the woman's bed had been torn and tossed.

Alex bent to right one of the baskets, but the woman touched her arm. "I will clean later. For now, I will take you to my brother. He will hide you until morning. But then you must leave our village. The Islamic State will return. They are searching for an American soldier and a woman with long black hair. They are searching for you."

Alex's heart dipped into her belly. The militants weren't going to give up until they found her and Jake. "We should leave now," Alex said.

"No," the woman said. "We have had troubles with the lions at night. They have discovered a taste for human flesh."

A shiver rippled down Alex's spine.

"I have a gun," Jake said. "We can protect ourselves."

"And if ISIS hears your gun, they will find you, kill you and leave your bones for the lions." The woman shook her head. "The morning will be soon enough. My brother has a truck. He can take you to the nearest town. From there, you will be on your own."

Hope surged inside Alex. A ride to the nearest town would be heaven. As long as the truck made it past the militants without alerting them to the passengers inside.

Then again, Alex wasn't so sure a ride in a truck was such a good idea. However, she wasn't sure she could continue on foot, either. Even staying the night in the village held an element of danger.

She held out her hand to the woman. "What is your name?" Alex asked. "I want to remember the woman who saved us from ISIS capture."

"Sabra," she said. "My name is Sabra. My brother is Kirabo."

"Thank you, Sabra," Alex said, and hugged the woman.

"I learned to read and write from an American missionary," Sabra said. "We welcome those who come to help, and protect them from those who want to harm our people."

They were led through the village to a hut on the very edge, farthest away from the road and set back from the other huts. Jake held her hand through the narrow streets.

Alex took comfort in the gesture. She figured she could survive just about anything, as long as Jake held her hand.

JAKE KEPT ALEX close by his side as they maneuvered through the streets to the hut on the outer edge. A barefoot dark man, dressed in what appeared to be a long white shirt, emerged from the hut and hurried to greet them.

Sabra nodded to the man and turned to Jake. "This is Kirabo. He will help you to the next town."

Before Jake could thank Sabra, she disappeared back the way they'd come.

Kirabo flung open the door to his hut and waved them inside.

Jake entered after Alex and turned to face Kirabo. "We can leave tonight, if you prefer."

Their host shook his head. "You will only become food for the lions, or target practice for ISIS. You will remain here until morning when I drive to the market in Ouallam. From there you can contact your people."

Jake nodded. "Thank you for your help and hospitality. We are truly grateful."

Kirabo clasped his hands together. "I leave you now. If we are visited again by the men who came earlier, I will alert you."

"Will that give us time enough to leave?" Jake asked. "We don't want you or anyone else to suffer because you helped us."

A flash of white teeth was Kirabo's response. "We have guards standing watch all night. We knew when you approached our well. Sabra insisted on helping you. Otherwise, we would have left you to the lions. There is food in the basket. My sister made it today. Eat. You will need your strength tomorrow." With that, Kirabo left the hut, closing the door behind him.

Darkness surrounded them.

Jake found his flashlight, switched it on and, using the red lens, shined it around the room.

A pile of tattered blankets lay in one corner, and a basket sat on a small rickety table.

Alex crossed to the basket, removed the lid and raised a crusty round disc. "Ah, bread." She lifted it to her nose and inhaled, closing her eyes. Her stomach rumbled loudly and she laughed. Then her smile faded. "Do you realize how precious this loaf of bread is to these people?" She laid the loaf back in the basket and covered it. "I can't take their food."

Jake frowned. "You need to eat to keep up your strength."

She shook her head. "I can't. They need it more. Besides, we're heading back to civilization tomorrow."

Jake handed her the flashlight and removed the cover from the basket. "At least take a small piece." He tore off a chunk of the bread and handed it to her. "We don't know what will happen tomorrow, much less tonight."

Alex stared at the proffered piece of bread, and her belly rumbled again. "Promise me we will return the favor soon?" She shifted her gaze from the bread to Jake's eyes.

"I promise."

Alex sighed, took the bread and bit into it. She closed her eyes and moaned as she chewed.

Jake's groin tightened. To keep from focusing on the way Alex was enjoying the morsel, Jake took another hunk of the bread and replaced the remainder in the basket. The bread was hard and crusty, but after over twenty-four hours of being on the run, it was heaven.

He savored every bite, chewing slowly before swallowing. When he'd finished, he realized he could have eaten the entire loaf, but, like Alex, he couldn't deprive the people who'd sheltered them of food that was so hard to come by.

He crossed to the bundle of blankets on the ground. "It's not the Ritz, but it's better than sleeping with the lions." He shot a smile toward the woman who'd kept pace with him since they'd left the village the day before. "Alexandria, you can have the first shift of sleep. I'll stay awake."

"Alex." She brushed the crumbs from her fingers and rubbed her hands over her arms. "The only person who ever called me Alexandria was my grandmother. I'm just Alex." She crossed to stand next to him, staring down at the meager pallet of blankets.

Jake nodded. "Alex, you can sleep first. I'm too wired to nod off."

"After what just happened in Sabra's hut, I'm still wound up, too." She drew in a deep breath and let it out slowly. "But we need to rest."

"Right. Tomorrow might not be as simple as Kirabo transporting us to Ouallam."

"True," Alex said. "We might run into more ISIS fighters. In which case, we'll be on the run again." She shoved her hand through her hair and dropped to her knees on the blankets. "I'll give sleep a shot, though it would be a lot easier if I had something softer than the dirt floor to lay my head on."

"I can help you there." Jake shed his bulletproof vest, leaned his rifle against the wall and sat next to her, bracing his back against the mud-and-stick wall. "You can use me as your own personal pillow."

She eyed him. "I can't keep taking advantage of you like that."

His eyebrows hiked, and a smile tugged at the corners of his lips. "Why not? You seemed to sleep fine snuggled up to me last night in the cave."

Though he found it hard to tell in the dim light from the red-lensed flashlight, he could see that Alex's cheeks darkened with a blush.

"Maybe so, but I can't get used to it. You won't always be there for me to lean on."

His smile faded. The thought of leaving Alex didn't sit well with him. He'd gotten used to traversing the rugged Niger hills with her at his side, and he found her to be good company. She didn't complain, and, no matter how tired or dirty, she was still beautiful. What would it be like to spend time with her in a less stressful environment? Like a hotel room with a soft mattress and clean sheets?

His groin tightened again and he shifted to adjust his pants. He had no business thinking about bedding the beautiful teacher. She wasn't the one-night-stand kind of woman. Whatever man she chose to be with had to be there for the long haul. He'd have to want what she wanted: a home, family and children.

Though she hadn't told him that was what she wanted, he could tell by the kindness in her voice and her desire to help others. She'd been teaching orphans and had seen to their safety before going back to help her missionary friends. The woman had self-sacrifice written all over her.

As a navy SEAL, Jake wasn't the man for her. He would be away from his home base more than he was there. If he ever married, his wife would be alone more than she was with him. She'd have to raise their children by herself because he wouldn't be there to help. What woman would sign on for that kind of duty? Marriage should be a union of two people willing to share in the responsibility of taking care of a house and children. Navy SEALs, by the nature of their jobs, couldn't be 100 percent engaged in family. Their first responsibility was to their country. Family came second.

Alex sat beside Jake, leaning her back against the same wall. "I came to Africa for the adventure." She chuckled. "I got it and then some. What I didn't expect was to fall in love."

Jake stiffened, his heart skipping several beats before it raced on. All he could think was, Alex had fallen in love? With whom?

The pretty teacher leaned her head back against the wall and closed her eyes. "I fell in love with the children and the villagers who didn't ask to be caught up in the constant violence. I fell in love with their resilience and ability to smile and laugh even when things were at their worst. I fell in love with the way they made do with what little they had. They always had enough love for their children, and they cared enough to take responsibility for those children who'd lost their parents to violence or disease. I'm sure you've seen the same."

He nodded. "I've been in villages ravaged by war, where naked, starving children are crying for their parents and so hungry they can't remember the last time they ate."

"It breaks my heart." Alex turned to him. "I can always go back to the States, where I'm afforded the opportunity to work. I'll eat three meals a day and never have to worry about where my next meal comes from. I can escape the horror these people have to live each and every day. But they can't." She smiled a sad smile that touched Jake's heart. "I fell in love with their strength of mind and spirit. It made me realize how petty my own problems were and how fortunate I am to be an American. We take so much for granted." She leaned her head against his shoulder. "Thank you for preserving my way of life. I just wish I could do more. But what can one person do to change the minds and hearts of those who continue to ravage countries?"

"We all do the best we can," Jake said. "Each individual's efforts add up."

"Not fast enough to help these people now." She yawned. "Jake, you're amazing."

He laughed. "How so?"

"No matter what the situation, you make me feel safe." She yawned again. "Is it some navy SEAL mojo or something?"

"Or something," he said softly, and slipped his arm around her shoulders.

Alex pressed her face into his shirt and relaxed, her body molding to his. Soon her breathing became even and deep.

Jake eased her head down to his thigh and stroked her hair, wishing he was in that hotel room with the clean white sheets. He wanted Alex to be more comfortable when he made love to her.

The second the thought came to him, he stiffened. His job was hard enough without wishing for things he couldn't—no, shouldn't—have.

The sooner he got Alex back to safety, the sooner they'd part. Making love to the pretty teacher wasn't in the game plan, he told himself.

As the hours stretched toward morning, with Alex asleep on his thigh, Jake could think of little else. Finally he eased her off his leg onto the pallet of blankets and stood, stretching the kinks out of his muscles. Morning light would come all too soon. He had to be ready to move. Getting Alex to a safe location was top priority. Then he would find his way back to his team and get on with his life.

Without Alex in it.

Chapter Seven

Alex woke and blinked her eyes open to darkness. When she rolled onto her back, she could see the pale light from the stars shining through the open door of the hut. Two figures were silhouetted outside, talking in low, urgent tones.

Immediately alert, she sat up, pushed the hair from her eyes and strained to hear their words.

When she couldn't make them out, she stood and hurried toward the door.

Jake stood with Kirabo in the darkness, speaking quietly enough not to wake the other villagers.

"What's going on?" Alex asked, and shivered in the cool air.

Jake slipped an arm around her and pulled her close. "We need to load into Kirabo's truck before daylight."

Alex snuggled closer, drawing on Jake's heat. "I'm ready whenever you are."

"Good." Jake nodded to Kirabo. "Let us know when."

"Sabra will lead you to my truck. I must go prepare." Kirabo left.

A moment later, Sabra appeared, carrying a plastic jug of water. "You will need to drink. The day will be long and hot."

Alex took the heavy jug from her and carried it into the hut. Jake turned on his flashlight while Sabra found a bowl and a cup.

She poured the water into the cup and handed it to Jake. Then she sloshed water into the big bowl. "For you to wash."

Alex stared at the water for only a second before she pulled her hair back out of her face and secured it with an elastic band. The she scooped water in her palms and splashed it over her cheeks, eyes and forehead, washing away the dust and sweat from her trek through the hills. Once her face was clean, she scrubbed her arms and the back of her neck. If Sabra and Jake hadn't been in the hut with her, she would have stripped and washed the rest of her body with the meager bowl of water.

Finishing quickly, she stepped aside for Jake to have his turn at the makeshift bath.

"Thank you, Sabra," she said, feeling more human than she had a few minutes before. She'd feel even better if she had a toothbrush and a comb for her hair.

Jake washed his face and dunked his head into the water, scrubbing his hair clean.

Sabra handed him one of the blankets from the pallet on the floor to dry with when he was finished. He drank from the cup of water.

Alex downed an entire glass of the refreshingly cool well water that filled her empty belly for a short time. She hoped they reached Ouallam before the day was over and that they'd find food there. When they did, she'd make sure to send some back to Sabra with her brother.

When they were ready, they followed Sabra out of the hut and toward an old truck parked on the edge of the village.

The bed of the truck was loaded with crates and stacks of empty burlap bags.

"Where do you want us?" Jake asked.

Kirabo pointed to the back of the truck. "There is a gap between the crates. You and the woman will ride there. I will stack more crates around you. Hopefully, we will not be stopped, but if we are, you will be hidden."

Alex planted her foot on a tire and pulled herself up on the side rails.

Jake gave her a gentle shove to help her over the top and into the truck bed. Then he climbed in with her.

The space Kirabo had left for them was tight, barely enough room for two people to sit with their legs pulled up to their chins.

But Alex wasn't complaining. At least she wasn't walking all the way to Ouallam.

As soon as Jake and Alex were in place, Kirabo shoved heavy crates around them and piled a lighter one on top, closing them in.

Moments later, the engine rumbled to life and Kirabo drove the truck out of the village. Night eased into day with light finding its way through the cracks between the crates.

Traveling the rutted dirt road while sitting on the hard metal truck bed wasn't luxury transportation, but it beat hoofing it on foot.

Several miles passed in silence.

"Are you all right?" Jake asked.

Alex nodded and rested her chin on her knees. "I'm fine."

The roar of the engine made conversation hard, but there was no other way to pass time unless she slept. "Did you sleep at all last night?"

"Too wound up," Jake said. "I didn't want to be surprised by another visit from ISIS."

A wash of guilt rushed over Alex. "You should have let me take a shift so that you could get some rest."

He shrugged. "I can function on a lot less. I learned just how much less during BUD/S training."

Alex had seen videos about the navy SEAL training conducted in San Diego, California. It was some of the most mentally and physically demanding training someone could go through. That Jake had survived and completed the training made him one of the best of the best.

"Why did you choose to join the navy?" Alex asked.

He rested his elbows on his knees and stared at the boxes in front of him, as if seeing the past instead of the rough wooden slats. "I needed to get away from home. My father wanted me to go to college and become a banker like him." Jake shook his head. "I was a good student. I could have done it, but it wasn't me. I couldn't be what my father wanted me to be."

"You had to be who you are," Alex stated. "I was supposed to marry my fiancé a year ago, when I realized I couldn't do it. He was the perfect man for me." She gave a crooked smile. "Or so my parents said. He had a steady job and would have been a good provider for me and whatever family came along." She paused, sure he couldn't possibly be interested in her pathetic excuse for a love life. Not when he had real life-and-death issues to deal with on a daily basis.

"But?" Jake prompted.

"He wanted me to stay in the same town where I grew up. He liked that we lived close to both of our parents."

"And that's a bad thing?"

It was Alex's turn to shrug. "Ever since I was old enough to understand the world was round, I've wanted to travel and explore this wonderful planet. I didn't want to stay in Virginia for the rest of my life."

"So he didn't want to leave Virginia. You don't have to move away to visit other countries. You can live in one place and travel to others on short trips."

"He didn't even want to do that. He was perfectly satisfied to limit our exploring to the state and national parks within a day's driving distance."

Jake chuckled. "So he was a homebody. Is that a crime?"

"No, it's not. And I'm sure there's some wonderful woman out there who wants the same thing as he does." Alex snorted. "She can have him. I wanted more."

Jake's eyes rounded. "You stood him up at the altar?"

She shook her head. "No, I left him the week before the wedding. I know it was poor timing, but I couldn't marry someone who wanted a different direction for our life than I did." Alex sighed. "I found the job with the missionaries and I left the day of my wedding."

"Ouch. That's harsh."

"I know, but it would have been much worse had I married him. I would have been miserable and would have made him just as unhappy."

"What made you finally realize he wasn't right for you?"

She tipped her head toward Jake. "Dinner the night before I called it quits."

"Dinner?"

"He didn't like that my fork kept tapping my teeth. He was raised by his mother and she had certain ideas about how a lady should behave. She passed those ideas down to her son. Apparently, clinking a fork against one's teeth is a social disaster."

"Did he question your manners about the fork?"

Alex's lips pressed together. "Yes."

Jake shook his head. "Your fiancé doesn't sound like the sharpest tool in the shed. What did you do?"

"I canceled the church and hall rental, broke it to my parents and fiancé, and signed up for a mission trip to Africa."

"And did absence make your heart grow fonder?"

Alex's lips twisted into a wry smile. "Just the opposite. Being here made me realize just how much I didn't love Paul and why it would never have worked between us. And it also made me realize how small and insignificant my problems were compared to what so many other people in the world have to contend with." She smiled at Jake.

"You made the right decision," Jake concluded.

"I did." A particularly big bump made Alex's bottom bounce on the hard metal floor of the truck bed. She shifted to relieve the soreness and ended up leaning more into Jake. He didn't seem to mind.

He slipped his arm around her shoulders to keep her from banging her back against the railing and continued their conversation. "Does that make marriage and family out of the question for you?" Jake asked.

"I don't know. I want to find someone who cares enough about me to look past my faults. If bumping my fork against my teeth is considered a huge liability… Well, you know. Why can't I find someone who likes to see different places, try different things, maybe even leave the States on occasion? Is that too much to ask?"

"Not at all." He laughed. "I'm sure there are plenty of guys who want to see the world and who aren't offended by the sound of a fork bumping your teeth."

She shot a sideways glance toward Jake. He was smiling. "When you say it, it sounds different."

"I've seen a lot of the world, but I haven't seen it all. There are so many more places I want to visit. Like Ireland. I've always wanted to go to Ireland. And Italy to see the Colosseum and Pompeii. And one of these days I'd like to visit Jordan and see Petra. I grew up watching Indiana Jones movies. Our world is more than just where we grew up."

"Exactly." She smiled. "My fiancé was content to stay in his own little corner of it. Well, I'm not."

Why couldn't she find someone who dared to be different? Someone who'd chosen his own path, not settling for the path that was expected of him?

All these thoughts roiled around in her head as she sat in the cramped space, next to a man who knew what he wanted out of life and had chased his own dreams to get it.

"So, you jumped at the chance to go to Africa." Jake's lips curved. "Were you aware of the unrest in many of the African nations?"

Alex nodded. "We were briefed on Niger and the factions functioning within its borders. I guess we were naive to think nothing would happen to us."

"Well, you weren't the only ones." Jake's lips twisted. "We were surprised that ISIS had made it as far west as your village."

Alex leaned into Jake's side, glad he had been at their village when ISIS came to call. "Thank you again for saving me from the ISIS militants."

"You're welcome. But maybe we shouldn't count our chickens until we get to Ouallam."

As if to prove his point, Kirabo slammed on his brakes, bringing the truck to a halt.

Jake's arm tightened around Alex, and he pressed a finger to his lips.

A male voice demanded Kirabo get down from the truck.

Alex huddled against Jake's side, her pulse beating so hard and fast against her eardrums she could barely hear.

Beyond their little cave of crates, someone was harassing their driver.

The truck bed leaned slightly toward the driver's side and someone grunted. From what Alex could deduce, a man had climbed up the side rails and dropped down on one of the crates. The cracking sound of wood splitting made Alex jump. She swallowed a gasp and held her breath.

The man on top of the crates was searching through them.

Alex captured Jake's gaze, her eyes wide.

He dipped his head and pressed a kiss to her forehead, followed by one to the tip of her nose.

His lips felt warm, soft and beautiful, distracting Alex from what was going on over their heads. She lifted her chin and met Jake's lips with her own. If ISIS killed them that day, at least she would have known the kiss of the navy SEAL.

She would have no regrets.

JAKE HADN'T MEANT to kiss Alex, but when she'd looked up at him with fear in her eyes, all he wanted to do was calm her and reassure her that they'd be all right. One kiss to her forehead led to one on her nose. When she lifted her face, he couldn't resist.

He kissed her lips, long and hard, pushing his tongue past her teeth to tangle with hers. She still tasted of the bread they'd eaten the evening before.

While someone crawled over the top of their hiding place, Jake kissed Alex. He clasped one hand behind her head, deepening the kiss, while the other hand reached for the knife in the scabbard on his leg. He'd be ready should the person searching Kirabo's load discover them hiding. In the meantime, he had the person he desired in his arms, and she was kissing him back.

A crate lid was slammed back in place, and footsteps moved from one wooden box to another. Finally the truck bed shifted as someone dropped to the ground.

The door to the cab opened and closed with a sharp bang. The engine started and the truck lurched forward, continuing along the road in the same direction. After they'd been rolling for several minutes, Kirabo stopped the truck, got out and climbed into the back. He shoved the overhead crate to the side and stared down at them. "Are you okay?"

Jake nodded. He was more than okay. He'd kissed Alex. They hadn't spoken since, but he could still feel the warmth of her lips on his. "Who stopped you?"

"Armed guards from a mining company that operates in this area. They wanted to make sure I wasn't stealing from them."

Jake's eyes narrowed. "Was it Snyder Mining Enterprises?"

Kirabo nodded. "The Niger government has granted them permission to search for potential mining sites in this area."

"Search?" Alex asked. "But they're—"

"Not too friendly, are they?" Jake finished Alex's sentence.

"No. They have approached our village several times. Many of our men have gone with them with their promise of jobs. They haven't returned for six months."

"You've had no word from them?"

Kirabo shook his head. "None. When we asked Snyder's representatives, they said our men ran away. They have no record of where they went."

"Have you brought this to the attention of your local government?" Alex asked.

"We have," Kirabo said. "Our government has too many other problems with ISIS stirring up trouble and refugees crossing our borders. They don't have the time or funds to come to our aid. But these are not your problems. We will be in Ouallam in twenty minutes, and you will want to hide your rifle while in the town. You can put it in this box." He pulled the lid off a smaller cardboard box packed with straw and melons.

Jake disassembled the rifle into two smaller halves and buried the parts beneath the straw and melons.

Once the box had been sealed shut and tucked among the others, Kirabo shoved the crate back over their heads and climbed down from the back of the truck.

Soon they were on their way, bumping along the dirt road, breathing in the dust kicked up by the wheels.

"Snyder isn't searching for mines," Alex said.

"They're actively mining," Jake finished. "And using conscripted labor to get the job done. Otherwise, why the armed guards?"

"They weren't necessarily keeping people out," Alex said, "as much as keeping them in."

Though Kirabo's statement was correct, and

Niger's problems weren't necessarily Jake's and Alex's, Jake couldn't ignore what they'd seen. When he reunited with his team, he'd share the photo and its coordinates with his commander and let the folks higher up in the food chain decide what to do with the information.

In the meantime, the truck slowed.

By the sounds of other engines and shouts from passing people, Jake guessed they'd arrived in a town. Until they pulled to a complete stop, he wouldn't know what town. He hoped it was Ouallam and that he would soon find his brothers, his team.

Chapter Eight

When Kirabo stopped the truck and climbed up in the back to remove the crates, Alex could barely move. She'd been crammed into the tight position for so long her muscles seemed to have forgotten how to function properly.

Jake was up first, reaching back to extend a hand to her.

She took it gladly and let him pull her to her feet.

The bright sunlight blinded her momentarily, and she blinked until she could focus on where she was.

Jake jumped down from the truck bed and held his arms up for Alex.

She sat on the edge and leaned into Jake's outstretched arms. He lifted her by the waist and set her on her feet, engulfing her in his embrace.

She held on to him until her legs steadied

and her muscles responded. Reluctant to move away, she turned in the curve of his arm and faced their driver.

Kirabo stood on the ground beside the truck where he'd parked it in front of an official-looking building. "This is the police building. They will help you to find your people." He set the cardboard box containing the melons and rifle on the ground at Jake's feet.

Jake shook hands with Kirabo, and Alex hugged the man, thanking him.

Kirabo left them standing in front of the building and drove away.

Alex prayed he'd be all right and that none of the ISIS folks or the people from Snyder Mining Enterprises had seen him drop off his human cargo. She didn't want him to suffer any repercussions for helping them escape. Unfortunately, he'd left in such a hurry, Alex hadn't had the opportunity to load his truck with food for his family.

Standing in the bustling town of Ouallam made the madness of the ISIS militants seem far away.

Jake lifted the box and tucked it beneath one arm. He took Alex's hand with his other and walked with her toward the building.

Before they stepped through the door, Alex

pulled him to a halt. "We can't take this box in there."

With a frown, Jake nodded. "You're right. But I can't leave it out on the street. Someone could take it."

"I'll stay outside with the box."

Jake shook his head. "I can't leave you and the box outside on the street. We'll have to risk taking it inside. As long as they don't have metal detectors, we should be all right."

"Great. And if they do?"

"Then I'll stay outside while you go in and ask to use the phone." He winked. "I'm betting they don't have the funding for expensive metal detectors."

"Maybe not, but they might want to check what's inside the box."

"And all they will see is melons."

"Let's hope that's all they see," Alex said.

Jake carried the box through the door and into the police building, walking with a confident swagger.

Alex stood back as Jake set the box on the floor and asked to use a telephone to make a collect call.

Jake cooked up a story about being an American soldier assigned to train the Niger forces. It wasn't the truth, but the facts might stir up the locals. He explained that his team had been attacked by rebel forces and he'd been separated from his unit, which wasn't a lie.

No one questioned the box on the floor. The man behind the desk asked Jake a few questions and checked with his supervisor, who came out from a room in the rear of the building to run his gaze over Jake.

Finally they agreed to let Jake use the phone, and he was able to call back to his base in Djibouti. Within seconds he was on the phone with his commander, giving his location and asking about the rest of his team.

The visible relief on Jake's face let Alex know his team had made it out of the hot zone intact. The smile he turned toward Alex lit up the room.

He cared deeply about his brothers in arms, and he must have been worried about them the entire time he was working to get her back to a safe place.

When he ended the call, he pulled her into his arms and kissed her soundly on the lips.

She laughed. "What was that for?"

"My guys made it out." He grinned. "We're going to be okay."

She cupped his face and asked, "Were you in doubt? Because if you were, you never let on."

"You never know what's going to happen in a foreign country."

For a moment, Alex basked in Jake's joy at the news that his men were fine. "So, what's the plan?"

"The good news is that my team is in the capital city of Niamey. My commander has been in contact with them. They're arranging for our transport to Niamey as we speak. Someone should be here to pick us up within the next two hours."

"And in the meantime?"

"We find food." He led her out the door with the box tucked under his arm.

"Way to woo a girl," Alex said. "Nothing says you care like offering a woman food."

"Right. And nothing says a man cares like riding with a beautiful woman in the back of a truck, squished into a place only big enough for a child for two hours."

"After two days without a bath or shower?" Alex laughed. "You must be so hungry you're hallucinating."

"No." Jake took her hand and brought her to a stop. "I'm serious. You're an amazing woman. I don't know any other female who would have made that trek without crying every other step."

"You underestimate most women," Alex argued, though she was touched by his words.

"Not the ones I've known." He cupped her cheek. "You're special, Alexandria. Don't ever settle for less than what you want. You deserve more."

She stared into his eyes, her heart swelling at not only his words but the sincerity of them shining in his eyes. "Okay. I won't settle for less than what I want. And right now, I want food."

A smile curled the ends of his lips. "Then food you shall have. The man at the desk told me about a café around the corner with the best food in town."

"And you have something with which to pay for said food?" Alex tapped the pockets of her jeans. "I left all of my possessions back in the village overrun by ISIS. The only thing I have going for me is my passport." She pulled it out of her back pocket. "And only because I keep it on me at all times, a lesson learned from my mentor, Reverend Townsend." Her smile faded as she thought about the good reverend and his wife.

"You couldn't have helped them. The place was swarming with militants."

Alex nodded. "I know. I hope they made it

out. When we get to Niamey, I want to see if we can get someone to help me find them and bring them to safety."

"I'll help you as much as I can," Jake said as he led her down the street and around the corner of a building.

"Thank you," Alex said. "You've already helped me so much. I don't think I can ever repay you for saving my life."

"No payment required. It's what I do. And this must be the place."

They stopped in front of a building with bistro tables set outside, umbrellas shading the seats from the sun.

As if they were tourists on vacation, Jake held Alex's chair until she took her seat. Then he rounded the table and sat beside her, his back to the wall of the building.

Alex stared out at the people passing in the street, a little on edge—understandably, she thought—after having the village she'd lived in peacefully for so many months taken over by dangerous rebels.

A man dressed in a white shirt and dark trousers stepped out of the building to take their order. He recited what was on the menu, as no menus were available. The fare was limited and Alex wasn't exactly sure what the items were, but at that moment, she'd eat shoe leather and be satisfied to have something in her empty belly.

She let the waiter choose for her and asked for bottled water to drink.

A few minutes later, the waiter returned with the water and two bowls full of some kind of soup or stew consisting of fish, vegetables, onions and spices.

Alex dug into the meal, amazed at how good it was. She and Jake didn't talk until they had finished every last bite. The waiter returned, cleared their bowls and set plates of some kind of kabob in front of them.

The succulent chunks of meat melted in Alex's mouth. By the time she'd eaten two of the kabobs, she couldn't swallow another bite.

When they'd finished their meal, Alex could only sit back in her seat and groan. "That had to be the most wonderful food I've ever eaten."

Jake patted his flat belly. "Agreed. Now we should be heading back to the police station. Our ride will be expecting to collect us there." Jake pulled a wad of local currency out of his pocket and laid some of it on the table.

"Where did you get that?" Alex asked.

"We always carry the currency of the area, in case we get stranded."

"Smart." With a full stomach, all Alex wanted to do was take a nap. After two nights of little sleep, she wished she could crawl onto a flat spot on the ground and close her eyes.

When they returned to the police building, they were met by a large dark SUV.

Five men climbed out and engulfed Jake in bear hugs.

A tall man with black hair and brown eyes clapped him on the back. "Man, you're a sight for sore eyes."

Jake grinned. "You have no idea how good it is to see all of you."

"We thought for sure you were dead," said a slightly shorter man with a stalky build and a broad barrel of a chest.

An auburn-haired man with blue eyes stepped in and clasped Jake's forearm. "We've had a drone flying over the village, but couldn't spot you nearby."

"Because we headed straight into the hills." Jake turned to Alex. "I met Alex in the village right before we had to make a run for the hills. She and I have been hoofing it through some pretty rugged terrain, chased by the guys who ruined our day."

"No kidding?" A man with brown hair and blue eyes stuck out his hand. "I'm Buck. Nice to meet you, Alex."

Alex shook his hand and nodded politely, slightly overwhelmed by the group of muscle-bound men.

The auburn-haired guy reached out. "T-Mac."

She shook his hand and turned to the shorter man with the barrel chest.

He nodded and took her hand in a bone-crushing grip. "Pitbull."

"Nice to meet you," Alex said and turned to shake the next man's hand.

"Harm," said a man with black hair and brown eyes. "Not that I'd do you any harm, but that's what they call me."

"And I'm Diesel," said the man who'd first hugged Jake. He shook her hand and back-handed Jake with his free arm. "Roughing it in the mountains, huh?" His lips curled into a sly grin. "I'm sure it wasn't all that rough with Alex."

Jake's brows drew together. "Alexandria was a teacher in that village. She worked with a missionary couple. She'd like to find out what happened to them. Any word on the status of the village?"

"None. Our contact via the Special Forces say al-Waseka's militants have set up security around the village. No one is getting in."

"Or out?" Alex's heart squeezed tightly in her chest. "What about Reverend Townsend and his wife?"

Harm shook his head. "We haven't heard anything about the missionaries."

"No word from al-Waseka concerning any ransom?" Jake asked.

"None," T-Mac confirmed.

"We've made contact with the American embassy in Niamey." Harm held open the door to the SUV. "They're expecting you to debrief them on what happened. We should get moving."

Diesel, Buck and T-Mac climbed into the rear seat.

Jake handed Alex up into the middle seat next to the man who introduced himself as Pitbull and then climbed in next to her. "What's our mission?"

"We're to stand fast in Niamey until intel digests everything. But we're to be prepared to mobilize if we're needed. We have a helicopter on standby with the closest Special Forces team."

"Good." Jake took Alex's hand in his. "We can't leave the missionaries to al-Waseka's mercy."

Alex shot a glance toward Jake. She hadn't expected him to express an interest in rescuing the reverend and his wife. He'd been clear that he was on military time and took his orders from them. Her heart swelled with hope.

"We also found something interesting in the hills," Jake added.

"What's that?"

"A mining operation that isn't supposed to be mining yet."

"Interesting. How close was it to the village?"

"Close enough." Jake's jaw tightened. "And at the last place we stopped, we discovered men had been taken by a mining company and promised work, and they haven't been heard from since."

"Conscripting?" Harm asked from the driver's seat.

"Could be," Jake said.

Alex's pulse kicked up. "You think what happened in my village has anything to do with the mining operation we ran across?"

Jake shrugged. "It seemed a little too coincidental that the villages surrounding the mining operations have been targeted by ISIS." He turned in his seat to face T-Mac. "Can we get the drones to do some scouting over the hills?"

"As soon as we get back to Niamey, I'll contact the drone squadron and get them on it."

Alex sat back in her seat, hope building inside. When she'd left the village, she'd thought for certain the reverend and his wife would be casualties to ISIS. But since no one had reported seeing their bodies, as gruesome as it sounded, they could be prisoners in need of a sharp SEAL team to rescue them.

Her only concern was that she wanted to be with them if they did decide to go after the Townsends. And she'd bet her last dollar Jake wouldn't allow it.

JAKE HELD ALEX'S hand all the way back to Niamey. Not long after they left Ouallam, she fell asleep against his shoulder and slept the entire hour and a half back to the capital city of Niger.

They didn't stop until they reached the gates of the embassy.

Jake woke Alex so that she could show her passport. Once the marine gate guard was satisfied by their identities and another had checked their vehicle for explosives, the gate was opened and they were allowed to enter.

Jake helped Alex out of the SUV and slipped an arm around her. "Just think, you're only a few steps away from a shower and a real bed."

"Almost heaven," she murmured.

"Just have to attend a debrief with the ambassador's staff, and we'll see about getting you some clothes and toiletries."

"Everything I brought with me to Africa is back in that village."

"I know. If the militants still have control, you won't be getting your things back anytime soon."

"And I need to call my parents and let them know I'm safe." Alex smiled. "Hopefully, they haven't heard anything about the village being overrun. Not much news from Africa makes it back to Virginia on the television stations. But my father reads online news and worldwide news sites. He might be worried."

"The embassy staff will help you with your phone call," Harm said. "All of that will have to wait. The ambassador wanted to conduct your debrief as soon as you two arrived."

Harm led them into the embassy building where staff members took Alex and Jake to a conference room. An army lieutenant colonel and a marine major were present, along with the state department staff. One staff member offered apologies for the ambassador, who was in a meeting with representatives from the African Union.

Alex gave her statement about what had occurred from the moment Reverend Townsend had entered her schoolroom and told her to evacuate the children to the point where she returned to the village to try to find the reverend and his wife.

Jake gave a brief description of how he and his team had been overrun by militants and how he'd rammed their truck to buy time for his team to escape. He continued the tale of finding Alex and their race through the hills to stay ahead of the fighters following them.

He stopped short of telling the group about the people who'd helped them in the town along the way or about the mining they'd run across in the hills. He didn't know why, but something inside made him keep that information to himself and his team.

Alex shot a questioning glance his way.

He gave a slight shake of his head.

Apparently, she got the message and didn't say anything to the gathering about the ride they'd received, the people in the last village or the mining operation.

Jake answered a few questions until he'd had enough.

Beside him, Alex sat straight, holding herself together, but he could tell by the dark circles beneath her eyes that she was exhausted and needed sleep.

Pushing to his feet, Jake announced to the room, "We'll be here for at least a day, and we've had very little sleep the past two nights. After we've rested, we'd be happy to answer any more questions. But, for now, let Alex and I take showers and find a couple of beds to sleep in."

The embassy staff excused themselves. On his way out, one man stopped beside Jake and Alex. "The ambassador would like to have a word with you tomorrow, after you're rested. Let me know when you're ready and I'll make the arrangements for you to see him. And so that you know, there is a reception tonight in the embassy ballroom. You and Miss Parker are welcome to attend, along with the other members of your team."

"Thank you," Jake said. "We'll let you know about the reception." He'd had it in mind to sleep through to the next morning, but if he could speak with the ambassador that evening at the reception, he might ask him about mining activities and the American companies involved in Niger.

How many people in Niger knew what was going on with the mining interests? Surely the American embassy had a finger on the pulse of all American corporations doing business in Niger, in which case the ambassador might know what Snyder Mining Enterprises was up to.

First, though, Jake needed to brief his teammates on what he expected to get out of the reception that evening. Until he knew more about what was going on in Niger with the mining and the ISIS attacks, Jake didn't want to share with the embassy staff all of the knowledge he and Alex had gained on their trek through the hills.

Knowledge could be power. It could also make him and Alex targets for someone who didn't want anyone else to know what was going on in the hills.

Chapter Nine

Alex was assigned a room next to the one Jake had been given. With no connecting door between them, she couldn't get to him without venturing out into the hallway.

After spending the past couple days with him in life-and-death situations, she felt bereft and exposed.

She told herself it was ridiculous, but she couldn't stop that feeling. They were in an American embassy, surrounded by Americans who'd sworn to uphold the constitution and protect people from their own country.

Then why didn't she feel safe? In the two days she'd known Jake, had she become dependent on the man? Now that she was away from him, all she could think about was when she'd see him again. Two days wasn't long enough for her to fall for a guy, was it? She'd spent six years getting to know Paul before she'd agreed to marry him.

Yet she'd taken only a couple of minutes to realize what a mistake that was and ended her engagement.

Falling for someone she'd known for two days was silly.

She gathered the bathrobe and travel-size toiletries and entered the bathroom. For the next fifteen minutes, she stood under the shower's spray, washing away the dirt and grime of the past forty-eight hours. No matter how long she stood there in the warm water, she couldn't shake a feeling of unrest.

Then she stepped out, toweled off and blew her hair dry, smoothing it with the brush that had been provided. She felt almost human.

One of the ladies on the embassy staff had given her a dress and open-toe sandals to wear, which helped with the guesswork of shoe size. She'd also given her a scarf to wrap over her head in deference to the culture of the area.

She could have put on the nightgown and gone straight to bed. After the debriefing and Jake's withholding of key information, she wanted to talk to him, to ask him why. An embassy staff member had escorted them to

their individual rooms, giving them no time
to discuss anything in private.

Now that she was bathed, dressed and feeling more human than before, she wanted to
talk to Jake. The man was on the other side of
the wall. So close, but so far.

Alex edged the door open and stepped into
the hallway. She had raised her hand to knock
when Jake's door opened.

She stood still, staring into his eyes. Her
own stung, embarrassingly close to shedding
tears. Why was she so emotional? They'd
only been apart for a few minutes, not days
or weeks.

Jake grabbed her arms and dragged her into
his room. Once she was over the threshold, he
kicked the door closed and backed her against
it, his mouth crashing down on hers.

Shocked by his desperate kiss, Alex opened
her mouth on a gasp.

Jake dived in, caressing her tongue with his
in a long, sensuous kiss.

She clung to him like a life preserver in a
stormy sea.

When at last he raised his head and inhaled
deeply, he pressed his cheek to the top of her
hair. "I don't know why, but it felt like the past

fifteen minutes was the longest stretch of the entire time I've known you."

Alex chuckled and rested her forehead against his chest. "I felt the same."

Jake smoothed a hand over her hair. "I wanted to tell you why I didn't say anything about the mining camp we ran into."

"Good." She smiled up at him. "Because I wanted to ask you why you didn't mention it in the debriefing."

"Harm came by my room. I told him not to mention the mining camp until we could find out a little more by doing some of our own sleuthing. T-Mac is a master at the computer. He can find out anything you never wanted revealed."

"What exactly are you looking for?" Alex asked.

"I want to know who is in charge of the Snyder Mining Enterprises activities here in Niger. Who owns it? Who does the owner have in his pocket to slide by the fact that they were supposed to be simply looking for places to mine, not start the mining operations?"

Alex nodded. "All valid questions. Still, why didn't you bring the embassy staff into your confidence?"

"I want to know these things before I talk

to them. What if they know what's going on and are turning a blind eye to it? They might attempt to cover up the problem rather than admit there is one."

Alex frowned. "What makes you think the embassy personnel aren't loyal, law-abiding citizens?"

"Nothing but a hunch."

"Will you at least clue in the ambassador?" Alex asked.

"Not yet." He stared down at her, holding her at arm's length. "If you're going to a reception tonight, you will need a cocktail dress."

"A cocktail dress in Africa?"

"You'd be surprised by the level of decorum the leaders strive for. I want you at the reception to listen for anything that might have to do with the mining and circumventing the Niger government rules and regulations. We also need to listen for anything concerning the ISIS uprising."

"Okay, I'll buy a new dress." She glanced down at the one she was wearing. "At least I won't have to shop in my underclothes."

Jake's eyes flared. "Now that gives an interesting mental image." He tipped her chin and stared down into her eyes.

For a moment, Alex thought Jake would kiss her again.

Instead, he sighed and offered her his arm. "Shall we go?"

Alex felt a flash of disappointment, followed by a warm feeling of being close to Jake.

In the lobby of the embassy, they met up with four other members of the SEAL team.

"Where's T-Mac?"

"He's on a borrowed computer, working his magic," Diesel said.

Harm leaned close to Jake and Alex. "He wanted to get all the information he could before the reception tonight. One of the staff members here showed us the guest list and told us who's who of the invitees. You'll want to be there. Hell, we'll all want to be there."

"Who's coming?"

"Mohamed Rafini, Niger's president."

"Nice. And they're letting us in?" Jake smirked.

"That's not all," Buck said. "Several National Assembly members will be here, along with some bigwigs from prominent corporations doing business in Niger."

"Anyone from Snyder Mining Enterprises?"

Harm crossed his arms over his chest. "As a matter of fact, yes. Quinten Philburn, CEO of

Snyder Mining Enterprises. He's had an office in Niamey for over a year, negotiating mining speculation projects with the Niger trade commission."

"He might be the one causing all the unrest in the area," Jake said. "If he's conscripting men to do his mining, he's a problem."

"True." Harm's brows formed a V over his nose. "But is he *our* problem?"

Jake knew what Harm was saying. But with Alex standing at his side, the voice of reason and empathy, he had to measure each word carefully. "If the ISIS attack has anything to do with the mining operations, yes. We were attacked. The missionaries, who are American citizens, were attacked. We have an obligation to our countrymen to help them when they're in trouble. So, yes, he is our problem."

"The CO will have to agree on that." Diesel lifted his chin and stared at his teammates through narrowed eyes. "We can't conduct unauthorized missions in a foreign country without stirring up a hornet's nest with our higher-ups."

Jake's lips pressed into a thin line. "Since when has that stopped us from doing whatever it takes to make things right?"

"He's right," Pitbull said. "When Marley

was in trouble, we didn't hesitate to help even though we weren't authorized to."

"And when the All Things Wild Resort in Kenya was targeted, we didn't back away. We engaged...without permission."

With a chuckle, Jake nodded. "That's right. We just have to be smart about it."

"And by 'smart,' you mean get permission from the CO?" Diesel prompted.

"Sure," Jake said. "Even if it's after the fact."

"That's not permission," Harm said. "That's forgiveness."

"Right now, we have to get outfitted for a formal party." Jake glanced around at his buddies. "How many of you have worn a suit in the past half century?"

"I wore one when I was seven to my great-aunt's funeral," Harm admitted.

Jake snorted. "Like I thought. We all need some threads to blend into the crowd tonight. We can't look like something the cat dragged in. Right, Pitbull?"

"Hey." Pitbull leveled a lethal stare at Jake. "No cat is going to drag this dog anywhere. And what do I need with a suit?"

Alex swallowed a chuckle at the look on Pitbull's face.

Jake went on to say, "Think of it as practice for when you boneheads marry your ladies."

Pitbull's eyes lit up. "Now you're talking. Though I think Marley would wear her flight suit to the wedding instead of a dress. And she's damned sexy in that flight suit. I think that's the first thing I noticed about her."

"No way. The first thing you noticed about Marley was her plane and how it made you all jittery inside." Harm clapped a hand to Pitbull's back. "Come on, even Marley would appreciate a tailored suit on her man."

The men laughed and headed for the embassy exit and the borrowed SUV.

Alex enjoyed how they poked and prodded one another. She could sense the tight bond between these men who lived, played and fought as a team. Never having had friends as close as the men were to each other, she envied their camaraderie.

Any woman who married into the group would have to understand their relationship was number one; their loyalty to country would come first, family second. But she had no doubt anyone these men loved would be loved fiercely, like everything else they did in life.

As she slid into the SUV beside Jake, Alex

studied the man who had never married. Perhaps he took his duty to country so seriously he would never choose a woman over the navy. Many men in the military found a way to have both. And many ended up divorced. The secret to the successful unions was the ability to adapt. Both partners in the relationship had to come in strong and stay strong throughout. They had to trust that each would be there for the other if the going got tough. *When* the going got tough.

Alex didn't have any long-term expectations of Jake. Yes, he'd kissed her, but he hadn't declared an undying love for her, and she wouldn't expect it so soon after they'd met. But the girl inside her that always read the books with the happy endings wanted to see Jake have his happy ending. And she wanted one of her own.

THREE HOURS LATER, Jake, Alex and the men returned to the embassy, having found appropriate clothing for the reception that evening.

Alex disappeared as soon as they returned, claiming she wanted to get a nap in before the party. He suspected she was excited by the dress she'd found. That she hadn't shown it to him indicated she wanted it to be a surprise for him.

Warmth spread through Jake's chest and heart. He'd offered to escort her to the ball, and she'd accepted with a brilliant smile.

"Where's T-Mac working?" Jake asked.

"In another wing," Buck said. "He and I are sharing quarters."

"Let's find out what we've been missing," Jake said.

Buck led the way to the wing of the embassy where he and T-Mac had been sharing a room. When he threw open the door, T-Mac barely glanced up from his computer. "Hey," he said.

Jake entered the room and held the door for the others to come in before he closed it behind them. "What have you found?"

"Some interesting connections," T-Mac replied.

"Really?" Jake leaned over the back of T-Mac's chair. "Like what?"

"I looked up Snyder Mining Enterprises and traced it back to its mothership, the Transunion Mining Corporation. At least, it was a part of Transunion until a year ago, when its assets were sold to a corporation out of Colorado. I'm having a hard time tracing the Colorado corporation. Its base is somehow buried in the

Cayman Islands. It might take me longer to sift through the data there."

"Interesting." Jake tapped the side of his cheek.

"I did some checking on our man Quinten Philburn, the CEO of Snyder Mining Enterprises here in Niger," T-Mac added. "He's got a pretty checkered past. He was fired from his job as chief operations officer at Rocky Point Mine in Alaska when the company was sued by indigenous people for polluting the nearby lake and river. Before the lawsuit, Philburn had a record of the most profits for any mining company in the area. After the lawsuit, the company folded and filed for bankruptcy."

Jake snorted. "Fired for taking advantage of the resources in America, yet he's working here in Africa, pretty much unregulated. We saw some of the men working that mine. The conditions were unenviable."

"Sounds like Philburn is squeezing as much of the profits as he can out of the operation." Harm spun away from the computer and paced across the room and back. "But, again, it's not our job to police the actions of civilians, even if they are from the US."

"No," Jake said. "It's not our job, but US citizens are in danger. We've been on missions to rescue Americans held hostage in foreign countries. It happens."

"It happens when the orders come from higher up," Harm reminded him.

"One other thing I found..." T-Mac turned in his chair. "Ambassador Brightbill had shares in Transunion Mining Corporation back before he joined the State Department."

"Does he still?" Jake asked.

T-Mac shook his head. "I couldn't find a current connection." He raised his hands. "That's all I have so far. But I'll keep digging."

"Thanks." Jake straightened. "I need to get ready for the reception. If all the players are there, I want to get a feel for who we're up against."

"Assuming we're up against anyone," Diesel cautioned. "We don't have clearance to go after the missionaries."

"If we don't get the clearance, I'm going without it," Jake said. "The sooner we go, the better chance we have of getting them out alive."

"I'm with Jake," Pitbull said. "They're American citizens. If they were my grandparents, I'd want someone like us to get them out of there."

"That's right," Jake said. "Think of them

as your grandparents. Would you leave your elderly grandmother and grandfather in the clutches of terrorists?"

Harm crossed his arms over his chest and glared at Jake. "You play dirty, don't you?"

Jake spread his arms wide. "I do what it takes."

Harm nodded. "You do." Then he clapped his hands together. "Let's go hunting. For information."

"And I'll stay behind and go through more data." T-Mac returned his attention to his computer screen. "Maybe there will be more connections that lead us to the primary source of issues."

"At least we have a good start on who to keep an eye on." Jake headed for the door.

Harm followed. "This evening's reception should be good."

"Counting on it." Jake opened the door and stepped out into the hallway. "I promised Alex we'd do something about her missionary friends. And I don't like to go back on my promises."

Chapter Ten

Alex couldn't wait to step out of her room wearing the beautiful ice-blue dress that matched her eyes and contrasted perfectly with her dark hair. The strappy silver sandals made her feel delicate and feminine after she'd spent the past few days hiking in the hills, smelling like a locker room and wondering when or where her next meal would come from.

Luckily the blisters she'd earned on the hike didn't hit any of the sandal's straps. She could stand in the shoes for a couple hours while she and Jake mingled with the guests, hopefully learning more about Niger and the location of the reverend and his wife.

If all else failed, Alex would go back to the village and ask the people there where the militants had taken the missionaries. For all she knew, the ISIS leaders might have taken pity on the Townsends and left them alone to care for the new mother and her child.

Alex snorted softly. "Fat chance." From what she'd heard, the ISIS group wasn't into charity or leniency. If the Townsends were still alive—her heart clenched at the other possibility—they were being held captive somewhere.

Smoothing a hand over her hair, she pulled the feathery-light, pale blue scarf up over her head, liking the way it made her appear even more delicate. Not that she was weak or terribly girly, but she relished the idea of others underestimating her. She saved her tough side for when she really needed it.

After one last glance in the mirror, she flung open the door and stared into the broad chest of a man standing there with his hand raised. She nearly had a heart attack until she realized it was Jake. When she got a look at him in a dark suit, his chin shaved and his hair slicked back, her heart palpitated a billion beats a minute.

The man positively took her breath away.

When she finally remembered to breathe, she looked up into his gray eyes. "Wow."

"I should say the same, but it would be completely inadequate to describe you." He took her hand and raised it to his lips. "You're stunning."

"You're not hard on the eyes, yourself." Heat

pooled at her core. She knew she looked good in the dress, but damn. She'd rather strip out of it, take Jake back into her room and make love to him.

Her blood raced, hot and fluid through her veins at the thought of getting naked with Jake. Two days? She felt as if they'd been together for much longer than two days. With all they'd gone through, it felt more like a lifetime.

She tore her gaze away from his and looked around his big body. "Where are your teammates?"

"The guys will meet us in the ballroom." He tugged on her fingers, pulling her enough that she had to take a step forward.

Alex laid her free hand against his chest, not to push him away but to balance herself when she was feeling so very off-kilter. The man made her experience so many different emotions, it caused her head to spin.

"Ready?" he whispered.

Oh, baby, was she. Alex nodded.

When he drew her arm though his and started for the stairs, she blinked several times and fell in step beside him, chastising herself for the idiot she was. Ready for what? To take him to her bed and make wild love with him? Was she out of her mind? They were strangers.

He was a navy SEAL; she was a teacher. He'd never spoken of anything between them that would last beyond when they went their separate ways. No commitment, no words of love.

Her breath caught in her throat and she nearly stumbled going down the stairs. They would eventually part, and the thought made her sad.

Jake tightened the arm holding hers, and he stopped long enough for her to regain her balance. "Okay?"

She nodded, heat rushing into her cheeks. Thank goodness he couldn't read minds. She'd be mortified if he knew her deepest, most sensual thoughts. What if he didn't think of her in the way she thought of him?

Naked.

She walked alongside him, proud to be with the gorgeous man, but conflicted on where they were going from there.

For now, anyway, to the reception.

Already the stately ballroom was filled with people dressed in their best clothing. Alex and Jake glanced toward the ambassador as they entered.

Alex had never been to such a grand event, and she was glad for the dress she'd purchased on Jake's credit card. She'd make certain she paid him back for the costly dress as soon as she could access her savings account back in Virginia. At least she fit in with the wives and female dignitaries. And the navy SEAL team did their country proud. Each man had shaved his beard and dressed in a suit and tie. They were handsome men who filled out the shoulders of their jackets like no other men in the room.

Jake, the tallest of his team, stood with his shoulders back, appearing like a Greek god lording it over his underlings.

Alex's chest swelled with pride when she had no reason to be prideful. He didn't belong to her. But he *was* her date for the night. She might as well enjoy it.

Jake met with his team. "We need to spread out, mingle with the guests and find the men we talked about earlier."

The others nodded and split up, blending in with the guests as much as handsome men could blend.

"What men did you discuss?" Alex asked.

"T-Mac had a list of people of interest. Like Quinten Philburn, CEO of Snyder Mining Enterprises. We also need to meet Ambassador Brightbill."

Alex frowned. "Is he a person of interest? Our ambassador?"

Jake shrugged. "There's a connection between him and the mining company. It's old, but it's a connection."

Alex nodded. "Okay. Philburn and Brightbill." She glanced around the room, studying the people. "The ambassador is still greeting people as they enter the ballroom. We won't get a chance to speak with him or even to shake his hand in the reception line. We'll have to wait until all of the guests have arrived."

"In the meantime, would you care for a drink?" Jake tilted his head in her direction, like an attentive date.

"I'd love one," she said, and laughed. "Two days in the hills with little water made me appreciate every drop I drink."

"What if there's alcohol?" Jake asked.

Alex shook her head. "I want water. Pure and cold. I think it'll be days before I feel any differently."

"Same here." He left her standing by a palm tree to walk toward the refreshments table.

Alex's gaze followed him all the way. Holy smokes, he was hot.

"I don't recall seeing you at any of the

functions," a deep, male voice said close to Alex's ear.

She jerked around to face a man in a charcoal-gray suit with salt-and-pepper hair and blue eyes. "Excuse me?"

He held out his hand. "Let me introduce myself. I'm Thomas Whitley."

"Alexandria Parker." She took the man's hand and gave it a perfunctory shake.

"As I was saying, I don't recall seeing you at any of the embassy functions."

"That would be because I arrived today." She smiled. "Do you come to all of the events?"

He laughed. "Most of them. I'm the ambassador's executive officer. His right-hand man."

"Then you would be at most of the functions. I would think you'd be in the reception line."

"Normally, I would be at the ambassador's side," he said, staring at the line of dignitaries greeting each guest as he or she entered the ballroom. "I arrived back from a trip an hour ago, and barely had time to shower and change."

"At least you made it in time to enjoy the party," Alex said. "Do you know most of the people in attendance, Mr. Whitley?"

"Please, call me Thomas." He glanced around

the room, his gaze pausing briefly on each individual, as if tallying the faces he knew. "Yes, you could say I know most of the people in attendance. Until I spotted you and the young man heading our way with refreshments."

Jake arrived with two glasses of sparkling water and handed one to her, freeing his hand to shake Whitley's.

"Jake Schuler," Alex said, "this is Thomas Whitley, Ambassador Brightbill's right-hand man, his executive officer."

"Call me Thomas." He shook Jake's hand.

"Thomas was telling me he knows just about everyone in the room," Alex said.

"That's impressive." Jake sipped from his glass and then nodded toward the room in general.

A man walked up to Whitley and started to talk about weather and growing seasons. When he paused in his diatribe, Thomas introduced him to Alex and Jake.

Since his wasn't a name mentioned earlier, Alex nodded politely, but didn't engage in conversation. Soon the man moved on to others in the room.

"Thomas." A man with dark hair and brown eyes, dressed in a black suit with a crisp white shirt, approached Whitley with a distinct and unwarranted swagger.

Alex imagined the man thought highly of himself, but she kept her feelings from being revealed on her face.

The man clasped Whitley's hand in both of his. "Glad I caught you."

"Quinten, what brings you to this neck of the woods?" Whitley asked, and pulled his hand free.

"We ran short on supplies on our mining expedition. I had to drive all the way in to Niamey to get what we needed."

Alex had to assume the man Thomas had called Quinten was Quinten Philburn, the CEO of Snyder Mining Enterprises. He was younger than Alex had expected. Probably in his midforties.

Whitley turned toward Alex and Jake. "Quinten Philburn, meet Alexandria Parker and Jake Schuler. They just arrived at the embassy today."

Quinten extended a hand to Alex first.

His grasp was strong, a little too strong, to the point it hurt Alex's hand.

She fought to keep from wincing. When he released it, she hid it behind her back to shake blood back into her fingers.

Then he turned to Jake and shook his hand.

The two men gripped hands for longer than the usual handshake. Jake's knuckles turned white before they finally let go.

"Where did you say you came from?" Quinten asked.

"We didn't," Jake answered, and turned to Whitley. "So, you work for the ambassador?"

"I do," Thomas said.

"How did that come about?" Alex asked. "Did he inherit you when he came to Niger to run the embassy?"

Thomas's lips twisted. "Not quite. We've been together for seventeen years. We go all the way back to when we both worked in the corporate world, prior to the ambassador's decision to join the State Department."

Alex raised her eyebrows. "And you both decided to work for the State Department?"

"After the dog-eat-dog world of corporate America, we were glad to dedicate our time to promoting our great country to others in the world." Thomas spread his hands wide. "And here we are, in the capital city of Niger, hopefully helping to make a difference."

"How altruistic." Alex softened the comment with a smile.

"And you, Mr. Philburn?" Alex gave him

her most innocent, questioning look. "What brought you to Niger?"

For a short moment, Philburn hesitated, his gaze boring into Alex's.

She felt a shiver of apprehension, but held her polite and—she hoped—questioning gaze.

"I came for the potential of profit." He glanced across the room. "Niger is a country with vast resources, much of which have yet to be tapped. That's why I'm here. To find those resources."

"And when you do?" Alex prompted.

Philburn captured Alex's gaze with a steady one of his own that seemed to look right through her to her innermost thoughts. "The Niger government will decide how they want to go about mining those minerals." He held her stare for a moment longer and then turned to Thomas. "I understand Niger's President Rafini is here tonight?"

Thomas nodded. "He is. And he will be in the capital city throughout the week."

"About time. I've been trying to meet with him for a month. He travels a great deal."

"Patience is the key when dealing with anyone in the government. The president is a very busy man."

"As are most people," Philburn snapped.

Thomas's eyes narrowed. "President Rafini isn't most people. As a representative of our great nation, I urge you to be cautious in your dealings with President Rafini."

Philburn snorted.

"You need to get with his people to schedule a meeting with the man," Whitley said.

"I will." Philburn nodded to Alex, ignored Jake and walked away.

"Ah, the reception line is breaking up." The ambassador's executive officer hooked Alex's arm. "Let me introduce you to my boss."

Whitley insisted on taking Jake and Alex over to where the ambassador was speaking with several people from the reception line.

As they approached, the ambassador glanced up and smiled.

"Thomas, who do you have with you? I'm certain I did not have the pleasure of meeting this lovely lady." The ambassador held out his hand. "And you are?"

Alex introduced herself to the charming ambassador, who was old enough to be her father and had a kind face. "Alexandria Parker. It's a pleasure to meet you, Ambassador Brightbill."

"Ah, Miss Parker. Thomas mentioned we had guests from the States staying in the embassy. I also understand you're here with a team of navy SEALs."

She nodded and turned to Jake. "This is one member of that team."

"Chief Petty Officer Jake Schuler." Jake held out his hand.

The ambassador reached out to shake it. "I'm told you and Miss Parker were involved in an unfortunate raid on a village east of here in the Tillabéri region."

Alex nodded. "We were, but Chief Petty Officer Schuler rescued me and brought me to Niamey."

"We are privileged to have heroes among us tonight," Ambassador Brightbill said.

Jake nodded without commenting.

"We have had difficulties with a certain ISIS faction in the Tillabéri region. Our US Special Forces are training the Niger army to defend itself against such attacks."

"But the people of the village were defenseless," Alex said. "There was no one there to protect them when the militants stormed their homes."

The ambassador's lips pressed together. "President Rafini is aware of the problem and is doing his best to build his army and their skills, with our assistance."

Alex bit down hard on her lip, wanting to tell the ambassador that what they were doing wasn't enough. But she realized the US ambassador couldn't always influence policy in Niger. That had to come from within.

In the meantime, her friends the missionaries were either being held hostage or dead.

When the ambassador, his executive officer and the CEO of Snyder Mining moved on to greet others, Alex drew in a deep breath and let it out slowly. "What am I doing here?"

Jake slipped an arm around her waist. "What do you mean?"

"I need to go back to the village and help the reverend and his wife. I'm wasting my time here in Niamey."

"You can't help them alone." Jake turned her to face him and held her hands in his. "I'll work with my commander. He'll chase it up the chain of command. We'll get a mission launched to rescue your friends."

"When?" Alex demanded. "After ISIS has used them as an example, tortured or killed them?" She shook her head. "Bringing it up through the proper channels will take too long. It will be too late by then, if it isn't already."

She lifted the skirt of her beautiful dress and spun on her fancy heels. The spacious ballroom seemed to close in around her. "I need air."

"Let me walk you to the garden."

"That won't be necessary. I'm going back to my room. I don't need you to escort me." She tugged to release her hand from his grip, but he didn't let go.

"Promise me you won't do anything tonight," he said.

She gritted her teeth without answering.

Jake squeezed her hand. "Promise."

Alex sighed. "Fine. I won't do anything tonight. But by morning, I'll find a car, a truck, whatever I can and head back to the village. I can't leave them to their fate. It's not right." She jerked her hands free of his grasp and spun on her heels, heading for the staircase leading up to their rooms.

JAKE WATCHED ALEX LEAVE. He hesitated for only a moment and then strode across the floor after her.

Buck stopped him with a hand on his arm. "Hey, buddy, where ya going?"

"Alex is going back to the village," he stated in a flat tone.

Buck's eyes widened. "Tonight?"

"I think I talked her into waiting until morning," Jake said. "But I don't know if she'll actually stay."

"Damn." Buck frowned. "You might not be able to stop her if she gets it in her mind to go."

"That's what I'm afraid of." He looked past his teammate as Alex disappeared at the top of the staircase. "However, I can go with her and try to make sure she doesn't get herself killed."

Buck touched his arm. "Dude, you can't go running around the Niger countryside. It's not safe."

"And I'm supposed to let Alex go off by herself?" Jake shook his head. "No way."

"You don't have clearance to leave. We aren't on vacation in here. The CO will count you as AWOL." Buck looped an arm over Jake's shoulders. "You need a better plan than taking off without guns, ammo or backup."

"Then come up with a plan while I make sure Alex doesn't go off half-cocked." He ducked out from under his friend's arm and hurried after Alex, praying he got to her before she left the embassy without him.

As he weaved through the throng of people there for the reception, he passed Quinten Philburn, Thomas Whitley and Ambassador Brightbill. Their gazes followed him.

He hadn't solved anything by being at the

reception that night, other than putting faces to the names of the persons of interest T-Mac had come up with. At least now he knew who was behind the illicit mining operations. Philburn didn't strike him as a man he could trust any further than he could throw him.

One additional piece of information he had gleaned that night was that Whitley and the ambassador had been together since they'd worked in the corporate world. He'd have T-Mac research Whitley along with the others.

What he still didn't know was whether the ISIS militants were roughing up villages on their own steam or if they were somehow connected with the illegal mining.

Jake didn't know, but he was sure T-Mac could find out given enough time. Only he wasn't certain he had time. His number-one priority for the night was to stop Alex from leaving to save her missionary friends. Once he made sure she was safe, he'd work on helping her to rescue the reverend and his wife.

Chapter Eleven

Alex hurried down the hallway and turned right at the corridor she thought led to her room. When she reached the end of the hall and hadn't found her room number, she sighed in frustration.

"Miss Parker," a voice called out.

She stopped and turned to find Quinten Philburn heading in her direction. Alex stiffened. The last thing she wanted was a confrontation with a man she was sure was conducting illegal mining operations with conscripted workers. After she found and freed the Townsends, she'd go after Philburn and Snyder Mining Enterprises.

Alex lifted her chin and started back the way she'd come, forced to face the man. "Mr. Philburn," she said as she moved to pass him.

He reached out, snagged her arm and pulled

her to a halt. "I'd like to have a word with you, Miss Parker."

"And you couldn't do that back in the ballroom?" She stared down at his hand on her arm and back up to his face. "Please, let go of my arm."

Instead of letting go, he squeezed tighter. "I don't know what you and your pet SEAL are up to, but don't be stupid and step into something you have no business meddling in."

Alex raised her eyebrows. "Whatever are you talking about?"

His eyes narrowed to slits. "You know damn well."

She tilted her chin in a challenge. "Perhaps you'd better spell it out for me."

The hand on her arm bit into her flesh, sending pain up her arm. When she tried to shake his hand free, he tightened his hold.

"I'll spell it out, all right." He jerked her around and pulled her back against his chest.

"Hey!" a voice shouted from down the hall.

Alex turned her head, relief rushing through her when she recognized Jake's stormy countenance.

Philburn released her arm and stepped away. "Things are different here in Niger. Just remember that." He stepped past her and strode toward the stairwell at the end of the hallway.

By the time Jake reached Alex, Philburn had disappeared through the doorway.

Jake wrapped his arms around Alex, lifted her chin and stared into her eyes. "Are you all right?"

She nodded, glad he was there, but not willing to let him know just how frightened she'd been.

Jake dropped his arms and turned in the direction Philburn had gone.

Alex grabbed his arm, her hand shaking. "Where are you going?"

He shot a glance back at her, his jaw tight, his eyes narrowed. "I'm going after him."

"Don't go."

He hesitated, one foot planted in the direction Philburn had gone, the other next to Alex. His fists clenched and unclenched while a nerve ticked in his jaw.

Then the muscles in his shoulders relaxed, and he slipped his arm around Alex. "I'll stay, but I'm staying with you tonight. I'll sleep on your floor, whatever, but I'm not leaving you alone." He pulled her into his embrace and crushed her to his body.

Alex melted into him, wrapping her arms

around his waist. She rested her cheek against his chest, the sound of his heartbeat thundering in her ear. "Lately, I get the feeling trouble follows me."

"If you're referring to me, you're right. I'm following you until whatever's going on is resolved. You can count on that."

"But you have a job to do." She tilted her head up to stare into his eyes. "You can't babysit me against *potential* threats forever."

Jake's jaw tightened. "No, but I can protect you now. Where's your key?"

She pulled the key out of her pocket and held it up.

Instead of taking it from her, he scooped her off her feet and carried her back down the hallway and stopped in front of her room.

Alex's heart raced as she leaned over to unlock the door.

Jake kicked it open with his foot, strode in and let her legs slide down his body. Still he held her against him, slow to release her. "Tomorrow, we'll do something about finding the Townsends. I promise."

"Thank you," she whispered, and leaned up on her toes to press her lips to his. "And thank you for being there when Philburn…"

Jake's lips thinned into a grim line. "Did he hurt you?"

"Not really," she said. There would be bruises on her arm by morning, but they would fade.

"What did he want?"

"I'm not sure. He more or less told me to mind my own business."

"About what?" Jake asked.

"He didn't say." Alex frowned. "Do you think he knows we've seen his operation?"

"It's possible." Jake smoothed back her hair from her face and then bent to kiss her forehead.

His lips were warm, soft and firm, making Alex tingle all over and long for so much more than a kiss on the forehead.

When he bent again to touch his lips to her forehead, she tilted her chin just enough to capture his mouth with hers.

Their lips touched, setting off an explosion of sensations throughout Alex's body.

He cupped the back of her head and held her closer, deepening the kiss.

She opened to him, sliding her tongue over his, reveling in his warmth and strength. After being with him every minute of the past few days, she'd missed him when they'd been apart for only a handful of minutes.

To Alex, the kiss became more of a frantic need to be close, to dive into him, to become a part of Jake. When he lifted his head, she dragged in air, her body pressing against his, fueling her desire, pushing her to the next level. "I want you, Jake Schuler."

"And I want you." He brushed his lips lightly across hers. "But I don't want to take advantage of you when you're most vulnerable."

"Oh, Jake. You don't make me feel vulnerable." She threaded her hands into his hair and brought his face down to kiss his lips softly. "You empower me." She slid her fingers along his neck to the tie knotted at the base of his throat. With deft fingers, she slipped the knot free and tossed the tie across a chair.

Jake chuckled. "Empowered?" He growled low in his chest. "I like the way that sounds." His hands skimmed up from her waist to her shoulders, located the zipper on her blue dress and dragged it halfway down her back.

Alex shivered in anticipation.

Jake halted before reaching the bottom of the track. "Say the word and I stop here."

"Good Lord, don't stop now." She reached behind her, covered his hand with hers and guided the zipper all the way down to the base of her spine. Then she hooked her thumbs into the lapels of his jacket and slid it over his broad shoulders and down his arms.

What happened next was a frantic effort to remove the remainder of the clothing between them.

Alex's pretty dress slipped off her body and over her hips, then dropped to pool around her ankles.

Jake bent to unbuckle the straps of her silver sandals and removed them with one hand on the shoe, the other on the back of her calf.

Heat built at her core, spreading outward to the tips of her fingers. Sure, she'd only known him for a couple days, but her body knew him as if they had been together for much longer. She couldn't stop the wave of longing, nor did she want to. Alex let it consume and push her to do things she would never have conceived of before she'd met him.

When Jake straightened, he rose slowly, dragging his fingers up her calf, along the inside of her thigh to cup her sex over the lace of her panties.

Her hands shaking, Alex worked the buttons of his shirt, loosening them one at a time.

When she reached the waistband of his trousers, he pushed her hands aside.

He had his shirt off in seconds, then toed off his shoes and stripped away his trousers.

When Jake stood in front of her wearing nothing but the smile on his face, Alex swallowed hard, her gaze roving his length, stopping on the jutting evidence of his desire for her.

Empowered, hell yes! She'd made him that hot, stirred him to such a proud erection. He wanted her as much as she wanted him.

Once again, he scooped her up, his arms cradling her nakedness against his. He laid her on the bed and parted her thighs. Inch by inch, he kissed a path from her ankle, up her calf, over the sensitive inside of her knee and along her inner thigh until he reached her center.

There, he parted her folds with his thumbs and blew a warm stream of air over her heated flesh.

Alex found it difficult to breathe. Her chest was tight and her gut clenched. She dug her fingers into the comforter and raised her knees higher, then let them fall to the side, giving Jake full access to the most sensitive part of her body.

He thumbed her there, tweaking the nubbin

with the tip of his finger. Then he dipped the finger into her channel, swirled it around in her juices and touched her nubbin again, stroking her until she dug her heels into the mattress and raised her hips for more.

Jake laughed softly and bent to take her with his tongue. He licked, nipped and teased that tiny bundle of nerves while pressing a finger, then two, then three into her channel.

The coil of her core tightened, pushing her up, up, up. When she reached the peak, she dug her heels into the mattress and rose with the surge that shot her over the edge. Alex cried out, "Jake! Oh, dear sweet heaven."

Jake continued with his sweet torture, holding her at that peak for longer than Alex thought imaginable.

When at last she fell back to earth, he climbed up her body and settled between her legs, his erection nudging her entrance. Then he jerked upright. "Wait."

"Wait?" she wailed. "How can I when I want you inside me now?" How could the man tease her when she was on the very edge of the most profound lovemaking she'd ever experienced?

He laughed as he dived sideways, rescued his trousers from the floor and pulled a foil packet from the pocket.

When Jake righted himself on the bed, Alex took the packet from his fingers, tore it open and rolled the protection down over him. Without pausing, she gripped his hips and guided him to her aching, dripping channel.

Jake took over from there, easing into her, letting her adjust to his girth before taking it all the way. He sucked in a deep breath and held steady, buried deep inside her. Then he pulled back out and slid in again, settling into a smooth rhythm that grew faster with each thrust.

His body tensed as he slammed into her once more and remained deep inside. His shaft shook in spasms as he spent his seed.

Alex lay against the mattress, her mind blown, her body deliciously sated and her heart already grieving the loss. Because when they went their separate ways, she'd never see this amazing man again.

JAKE DROPPED DOWN on top of Alex, gathered her in his arms and rolled onto his side, taking her with him. He maintained their intimate connection, reluctant to leave her body when he felt so right inside her.

She'd been every bit as passionate as he had, taking charge when she wanted more and giving him her all. Not only was she gutsy, she was beautiful and amazing in bed and out. How could he walk away from her when their mission in Niger ended?

He lay beside her, stroking her hip, her arm, her hair, memorizing how she felt beneath his fingertips. When they parted, all he'd have left were the memories of making love to her and hiking through the hills of Niger with her at his side.

"I'll miss you when this is all over," Alex said and yawned, her eyes drifting closed.

Jake smoothed a strand of hair off her cheek. "We can see each other again. This doesn't have to be the end."

Without opening her eyes, she gave him a sad smile. "I'll be somewhere in Africa, teaching. You'll go on to your next mission…"

He didn't want to think they would never see each other again. Now that he'd found Alex, he didn't want to let go. "You'll eventually come back to the States, won't you?"

"Probably, but I don't know when or where I'll land. You can't wait for me." She rolled into his side and pressed her lips into his chest.

"What if I want to?" he whispered.

She didn't answer. Slowly Alex's breathing became more regular and her pulse slowed as she fell asleep snuggled into his side, her cheek against his heart, her arm over his chest.

For a long time, Jake lay awake, wondering what the next day held in store for him and his SEAL team. Mostly he wondered where it would lead with Alex. He couldn't let her go back to the village.

He and his team could launch an extraction mission to recover the missionaries, but they'd need additional ammunition and support from the rest of the unit back in Djibouti. That would take time. He wasn't sure Alex would be okay with waiting for that support to arrive.

Somehow, he had to convince her it was the right thing to do. If not, he might have to go it alone. He wouldn't want to risk the lives of the small contingent of SEALs there in Niamey on a promise he'd made.

The more he thought about it, the more he convinced himself going in alone would be the answer. At the very least, he'd be able to assess the situation. If he could get the couple out without the assistance of his team, all the better. The trick would be to keep Alex from coming with him.

To do that, he had to put one of his buddies on her to hold her back. As he lay with Alex in his arms, a plan formed.

Well before sunrise, Jake pressed a gentle kiss to Alex's lips without waking her and then rose from the bed. He took the time to slip into his pants and padded barefoot around the room gathering the rest of his clothing. Jake exited the room, pulling the door closed as quietly as he could. He hurried to his room, shucked the suit pants and climbed into his freshly laundered uniform, impressed by how quickly the embassy staff had cleaned and returned the items. Dressed and ready before sunrise, Jake made his way to T-Mac's room.

His teammate answered the door quickly. Jake knew the man wouldn't have gone to sleep with so many questions still up in the air.

T-Mac shoved a hand through his hair and yawned. "What are you doing up so early?"

"I couldn't sleep." Jake stepped past T-Mac and his friend closed the door behind him. "I need you to do me a favor."

"Name it." T-Mac strode barefoot back to the desk where he'd set up the borrowed laptop.

"I need you to run interference with Alex and the rest of the team."

T-Mac frowned. "What do you mean?"

"I'm going back to that village to see if I can locate the missionaries. If I'm able to get in and get them out, I'll bring them back with me. If not, I'll return for assistance. But I at least want to put eyes on the target."

Before he'd finished speaking, T-Mac was already shaking his head. "No way. You can't go there alone."

"I can, and it makes sense." Jake paced the short length of the room and turned. "If I go alone, I can get in and out without being detected. If I'm caught, I'll say I went AWOL and tell them the rest of the team knew nothing about my reconnaissance mission back to the village. You will all be in the clear."

"Thanks, but I'm not as worried about what the higher-ups will think as I am worried that you will be caught and used as an example of what happens when US military gets involved in Niger affairs."

"It's a chance I have to take. I can't drag everyone else into this, and I can't sit around and wait until Alex takes matters into her own hands and attempts a rescue on her own."

"Are you going to do this whether or not I agree with it?" T-Mac asked.

Jake nodded. "I am."

"Then get going. I'll see what I can do to sit on Miss Parker."

"And keep the team from coming after me,

will ya?" Jake added. "This is my issue. None of you need to be involved."

"Uh, yeah." T-Mac turned away. "I can't make that promise."

Jake knew he was asking a lot of T-Mac. "Please. Don't let Alex follow me. And at least wait until I'm gone before you clue the rest of the team in on where I'm going. And if things go south, let them know... Well, you know."

T-Mac locked forearms with Jake and pulled him into a bear hug. "Don't stick your neck out too far. ISIS won't cut you any slack."

Jake didn't expect a promise not to do anything from his teammate; in fact, he anticipated T-Mac would notify his team before he had a chance to collect his weapon at the gate and find transportation back to the village. If he were in T-Mac's shoes, he'd do the same. He just prayed he wasn't leading them all into one hot mess of a confrontation with the ISIS militants. Without the supporting artillery and additional SEALs, they didn't stand any more of a chance than they had during the first altercation.

But, this time, he had the element of surprise on his side. Who would expect a lone SEAL to infiltrate a stronghold? The SEAL would have to be crazy.

Or crazy in love.

Chapter Twelve

Alex woke to the sun creeping in around the edges of the blackout hotel curtains.

She stretched languorously and smiled. That was what incredibly great sex did for someone. It made her wake up feeling rested and deliciously satisfied.

The pillow beside her was empty, but that didn't alarm her. She figured Jake was either in the bathroom or had gone next door to dress for the day, leaving her to sleep off the effects of two days in the hills.

She rose and took her time in the shower, letting the warm water wash over her skin. Her nerve endings were strangely sensitized to anything that touched her, reminding her of every inch Jake had kissed.

Once she'd dried her hair and dressed in her laundered jeans and the shirt she'd purchased along with the dress the day before, Alex left her room and knocked on Jake's door.

When she received no response, she knocked again, a niggle of irritation pulling her brow lower. She told herself it was okay. He'd probably gone to check status with his team or to find something to eat.

Alex went in search of the other men on the SEAL team. When she came to the corridor the other five men were staying on, she could hear voices behind T-Mac's door. With her heart soaring in anticipation of seeing Jake again, Alex knocked on the door.

The voices grew silent.

A moment later, T-Mac opened the door. "Alex, please come in."

She entered and smiled at the five men standing in the room that seemed far too small to hold their broad shoulders. Her smile faded. "Where's Jake?"

Four of the five men looked toward one. T-Mac.

The SEAL ran a hand through his hair. "Alex…" T-Mac started, cleared his throat and ran his hand through his hair again.

Her heart seized in her chest and she couldn't find her next breath.

Harm stepped forward. "We were just discussing Jake, trying to decide what to do."

"We can't just go balls-to-the-walls after him," T-Mac said. "We have to think through this issue and come up with a game plan—"

Alex sliced her hand through the air, cutting off T-Mac's words. "What issue and where's Jake?" She crossed her arms over her chest and stared at each SEAL one at a time, her eyes narrowing until they were no more than slits.

T-Mac sighed. "He left this morning."

"Left? For where?" Alex demanded.

"He's going to find your missionaries," Pitbull said. "He didn't want you to go off all half-cocked, so he did."

"Damned crazy if you ask me," Diesel said. "If he doesn't get himself killed, we're gonna kill him for being a jerk."

Her pulse pumped so hard against her eardrums she couldn't hear herself think. "Let me get this straight... Jake went back to the village to find the Townsends?"

T-Mac nodded. "For the record, he didn't want you to go after him." The SEAL looked at the rest of his team. "He didn't want any of us to go after him."

Pitbull slammed his fist into his palm.

"Well, that's bullshit. What kind of team lets one of its own go solo?"

"Not this team," Buck said.

"Damn right," Harm agreed.

"The question is, what are we going to do about it?" T-Mac asked. "He's got at least a two-hour lead on us."

"Five or six of us are not going to win a frontal attack on them. We have to launch a subversive attack, sneak up on them and surprise them."

Diesel nodded. "Yeah. We can't let them know we're coming. It gives them time to set up defense and repel our aggression. We have to hit them when they least expect it and run like hell to get away."

"I'm going with you," Alex said.

The room went deadly silent.

T-Mac held up his hands. "Jake wanted you to stay where it's safe. I more or less promised to make sure you stayed."

"Well, you'll just have to break your promise. Because if you don't take me, I'll find my own way back to the village—with or without your help."

"Alex, we can't bring you along. Having you there will be a distraction that could get one of us or Jake killed."

He had a point. But Alex wasn't going to stay back in Niamey twiddling her thumbs while Jake and his team marched into the village and demanded the release of Reverend and Mrs. Townsend. Waiting for news would kill her. "I know which hut they were supposed to be in. If ISIS left them alone, they might still be in that hut. At the very least, if they left the mother and her baby there, she might know where they took the Townsends."

"Then tell us where to look," Harm said. "But we'll be the ones to go into the village."

Alex shook her head. "The villagers might not talk to strangers. They will be frightened of repercussions from ISIS. If I can get in there… They know me, they'll talk to me."

"The answer is still no," T-Mac said. "Jake wanted me to make sure you stayed away from the village. He put me in charge of securing you."

Alex stared at T-Mac over her crossed arms. "And you think you can keep me from doing whatever the hell I want?"

T-Mac cast a glance at Harm. "You tell her," he said, and turned away.

"If you go after Jake, you put him and the rest of the team in danger. We'll be too busy making certain your life is not at risk to protect our own." Harm took her hand. "Think about it. If Jake discovers you there in the village, he'll lose focus and potentially get himself killed. Do you want to be responsible for Jake's death?"

Alex's mouth set in a grim line. "If Jake dies, it's his own damned fault for running off without getting proper backup." She lifted her chin. "Go ahead, plan your own operation. I have plans of my own." She walked to the door, turned and glared at the SEALs. "Whatever you do, get Jake out of there alive. That's all I ask."

She'd launch her own operation and fly solo.

Alex hurried back to her room, grabbed her passport and left again. She had some work to do to access her bank accounts and rent a vehicle. The embassy staff should be able to help her with the details. That was one of the reasons they were there. To help American citizens in trouble.

And if all else failed, Alex would steal a damned vehicle. She was going after Jake, come hell or high water.

JAKE WAS ABLE to borrow a vehicle from the embassy motor pool, promising to return it the next day. What he didn't tell them was why he needed it and that there was a strong possibility that he wouldn't return the SUV—or live to explain why. No one else needed to know that he was headed out on a potentially suicidal mission armed with a rifle, one magazine of ammunition and his trusty Ka-Bar knife.

He should be able to enter the village under the cover of night, find the missionaries and get them out without raising too much of a ruckus.

And pigs can fly.

All he could hope for was a miracle. He just couldn't wait around for Alex to make the same move he was attempting. She'd be in a much worse position as a single female targeted by ISIS. With him, he could fight back and they'd probably just shoot him and drag his body around for show. With Alex, they'd do a lot worse than kill her.

Jake got an early start, setting out before the sun rose in the east. He covered quite a few miles before the big orange globe arose from the horizon. For the next couple of hours, he squinted at the bright sun as he drove along the rutted road toward the very village he'd escaped from days ago.

Several times he was slowed by herds of goats or cattle crossing the road in front of him. He slowed and inched his way through. When he came within five miles of the village where the ISIS militants had ambushed them and where he'd subsequently met Alex, he pulled over a hundred yards off the road. In a copse of trees and bushes, he hid the SUV, piling branches and brush around it to hide it from anyone passing by. He would need to bring the missionaries back this way and have a vehicle to transport them away from their captors.

If he found them, if they were still alive and if he was able to sneak them out of the village.

If, if, if.

At a little past noon, he walked away from the SUV, moving through the trees and brush toward his goal. He wouldn't attempt to enter the village until nightfall, but he could scout out the sentries guarding the perimeter.

By now Alex would be awake. The guys would have told her he'd left, and she'd be in a lather to follow. He prayed T-Mac and the rest of the team were successful in keeping her from climbing into a vehicle and setting out on her own.

He couldn't think about Alex now. Finding the Townsends was his major concern, and he focused all of his attention on getting close to the village without being spotted.

When he spied the first hut on the edge of the small village, he squatted between the branches of a bush, brought his rifle to his shoulder and peered through the scope.

A few women moved about the village, herding children or cooking and preparing food. On the surface, everything appeared to be normal.

Then he spotted a man in black garb shoving an elderly villager in front of him. The gray-haired old man fell to his knees. His tormentor kicked him in the side and yelled at him.

The old man staggered to his feet and kept moving toward one of the larger huts in the center of the village.

ISIS was still in charge, and the villagers were under their command. So much for hoping they'd only hit the village and moved on. Apparently, they were there to stay, and the Niger government wasn't doing anything to change the status quo.

Jake couldn't make his move until dark settled over the village, but he could look at the situation from all sides.

Over the course of the next six hours, he made a wide circle around the outskirts of the village, counting eight guards positioned at intervals all around it. Most carried AK-47 model rifles. They leaned against trees or squatted on the ground with their rifles lying beside them in the dirt. Evidently, they weren't expecting much action.

Throughout the day, Jake looked for signs of the missionaries. So far, he hadn't seen them. But the good news was he hadn't seen any bodies, either. If the ISIS fighters had killed the elderly couple, they wouldn't have done them the honor of burying them. That wasn't their way. If anything, they would have found a way to parade them before the others as a deterrent against subversive behavior.

As the sun dipped low on the horizon, Jake settled into his position and memorized what lay between him and the village. He'd sneak in from the direction of the hills, the same way he'd gotten out with Alex.

As he waited in the shadow of a tree, surrounded by underbrush, a herd of goats ambled toward him, followed by a child of ten or eleven years old.

The herd paused to nibble on the bushes concealing Jake.

As much as he wanted to shoo them away, Jake remained still, hoping the goats and the child would eventually move on without noticing the SEAL with the gun hiding in the brush.

That was not to be the case. A particularly frisky goat kid bounced around the bush in front of Jake, nibbled on the leaves and poked his head through the branches, coming face-to-face with Jake.

Jake blew a stream of air into the kid's face, hoping to scare off the little pest.

The child followed the kid, reached in to pull the baby goat out of the brush and froze when he spotted Jake.

"It's okay." Jake spoke in his broken French and held up his hand. "I'm not here to hurt you."

The boy looked from Jake back toward the village where an ISIS sentry sat, sleeping against a tree. When he turned back to Jake, he eased away from the brush, pulling the kid with him.

"Do you know Miss Parker?" he asked.

The boy backed up another step.

What did they call Alex here in the village? Why hadn't he thought to ask her? If Jake didn't capture the boy's trust and attention in the next second, the child would take off toward the village and alert the ISIS militants of the man in the bushes. He'd have the entire group of ISIS fighters swarming over him in less time than it took for him to say *I come in peace*.

"Miss Alex sent me," Jake said. "The teacher who worked with Reverend Townsend and his wife. She sent me to help."

The boy stopped his backward progression and narrowed his eyes. "You know Miss Alex?" The boy spoke in English.

"Yes," Jake said. "I was with her this morning. What's your name?"

"I am Jolani. Miss Alex was teaching me to read and speak English. We love Miss Alex. Is she all right? Is she safe?"

Jake nodded. "She's in Niamey. She sent me to find Reverend and Mrs. Townsend."

Jolani glanced over his shoulder toward the sentry, who'd just woken from his brief nap in the heat of the afternoon. "You must go. If they find you here, they will kill you. Tell Miss Alex to stay away. It is not safe here."

"I'll tell her. But first, can you tell me if the reverend and his wife are still alive?"

The boy nodded, his eyes rounding. "He's coming," the boy said.

The sentry who had been asleep a moment before rose from the ground and started toward the boy and Jake's spot.

"I must go," the boy said.

"Please. Are the reverend and his wife alive?"

Jolani nodded and whispered, "They are being held prisoner in the biggest hut in the village. They are guarded by many ISIS men. You will not be able to help them. Go back. Tell Miss Alex not to come. She cannot help them."

"I'll tell her," Jake said.

But the boy had already moved away from the bush, herding the goats toward the man dressed all in black, blocking him from advancing toward Jake's hiding place.

Jake wished he could protect Jolani instead of the boy protecting him by diverting the militant fighter.

Hope swelled in Jake's chest. The Townsends were still alive. The next hurdle he faced was getting them through the gauntlet of ISIS soldiers to safety.

Chapter Thirteen

No matter how hard she tried to convince the embassy motor pool staff to loan her a vehicle, they refused, claiming they had to keep a number of the vehicles on hand for staff needs. They'd already loaned out two to various navy men.

Alex's fists clenched. "When did the men leave?"

"One before daylight. The others are just now loading up." The attendant called out after Alex's quickly departing figure, "They were in a hurry. They might already be gone."

Then Alex would run after them and chase them down. She'd be damned if they left her behind. That was her village and her friends being held captive. If she could help in any way, she would.

As she rounded the corner of the building,

an SUV pulled out of the motor pool parking lot.

Diesel was behind the wheel, and Harm sat in the passenger seat. The others were seated in the rear.

Without thinking beyond her immediate needs, Alex leaped in front of the moving vehicle.

Diesel slammed on the brakes, bringing the big SUV to a screeching halt, but not before bumping Alex.

The impact wasn't hard enough to hurt her, but she fell to the ground, forcing them to stop and check on her.

Diesel shoved the gearshift into Park and jumped out. "Alex, are you all right?"

All five of the navy SEALs were out of the vehicle, surrounding her.

Alex lay for a moment with her eyes closed, letting them think the worst. Served them right for excluding her from Jake's rescue mission.

When Buck bent down, rolled her onto her back and felt for a pulse, Alex grabbed his wrist and opened her eyes. "I'm fine, but you're taking me with you."

Buck glanced up at T-Mac. "She's all yours."

T-Mac shook his head. "Alex, Jake needed to know you wouldn't follow him. I promised I'd make sure that didn't happen." He bent down and reached for her hand. "Come on, Alex."

"I'm going with you guys." She took his hand to allow him to help her up.

T-Mac jerked her to her feet, doubled over and shoved his shoulder into her midsection.

Alex hadn't expected the move and flopped over onto T-Mac's back as he lifted her in a fireman's carry. "What the hell, T-Mac. Put me in the SUV. I'm going with you."

"Can't take you, Alex. A promise is a promise." T-Mac waved at the others as they climbed into the SUV. "Take care of Jake and let me know if I can do anything back here to help. As soon as you're out of communication, I'll place the call to the CO and see if he wants to contribute more assets to this mission."

"Thanks, T-Mac, for taking one for the team," Harm said as he climbed into the passenger seat.

"What did he just say?" Alex kicked and squirmed against the iron arm clamped around her legs. "Let me down."

"Not until the others are gone."

"I'll just find another way to get to the village. You can't hold me captive forever. The embassy staff will arrest you."

"Nope. I don't think so." T-Mac carried her

in through a side door of the embassy and climbed the stairwell to the second floor. Every time she tried to scream, T-Mac bounced her hard, knocking the air from her diaphragm.

They were in his room before she could draw attention to her plight, and, sadly, the others were long gone.

When T-Mac finally set her on her feet, she crumpled to the floor and gave in to the tears burning the backs of her eyelids. "I only wanted to help."

"You'll help best by staying out of it. Jake and the others need to focus on the job at hand. If you're out there, they'll be distracted from the mission." T-Mac booted up his computer. "You can help me convince my commander that the team needs additional support. He might take it better from you since you know the missionaries personally."

"Anything to help Jake and the others." She wiped the tears from her cheeks and rose from the floor. "Call him."

"I'll do better than that. I'll bring him up on video." T-Mac worked his magic with the laptop and a few minutes later, a man with short-cropped hair, wearing a navy camouflage uniform, popped up on the screen.

"T-Mac, give a current sitrep. I've got the

State Department breathing down my neck about the ISIS attack in the Tillabéri region. What more have you learned?"

"Sir, the good news is Big Jake was able to recover the teacher colocated with the American missionaries in the village where we were attacked. The bad news is the reverend and his wife are still missing."

"The State Department wants us to back down. They had a call from our ambassador in Niger. He's concerned our meddling will undermine the Niger forces and national government. We're to stand down and let their military handle the situation."

Alex's heart slid into the pit of her belly. Jake and his team weren't going to get any help.

"Uh, sir," T-Mac said. "I'm afraid it's too late."

The commander's scowl filled the screen. "What do you mean it's too late?"

"Big Jake and the others are on their way now to the village in an effort to extract the missionaries."

The CO cursed and pounded the desk in front of him. "Who the hell authorized the mission?"

"No one, sir."

"Sir, if I may interrupt." Alex stepped into the screen view.

"Who the hell are you? T-Mac, what's a civilian doing in a classified briefing?"

"Sir, this is Alexandria Parker, the American Big Jake helped to escape the village."

"Sir, Jake and the others are going after Reverend Townsend and his wife because time is of the essence. If we had waited for permission, they might not be alive to rescue. And if T-Mac and the others hadn't imprisoned me, I'd be with them now."

"Ma'am," the commander said, "I understand your concern, but what those men do is a reflection on the American military. The Niger president doesn't want us mucking around in his country. We have to respect his wishes. Otherwise, we might start an international incident."

"The reverend and his wife are American citizens," Alex argued. "We can't leave them to the mercy of ISIS. They're kind, gentle people who came to help the poor and sick."

"I understand. But they had to know the risks involved in coming to an African country," the commander said.

"Sir," T-Mac interrupted, "no matter what they want us to do, our men are going in and we don't have communication equipment to call them off. What can we do to make sure we don't have to collect them in body bags?"

Alex stared at the man on the screen. "Those are good men. Please tell me you're going to help them."

The commander sighed. "This better be the last time I have to bail out my men when they take matters into their own hands. I have a mind to redeploy you six back stateside. You're more trouble than you're worth at this point." He ran his hand over his face. "Here's what I'm going to do. It might be a little too late."

Alex released a sigh and listened to the plan. Then, while T-Mac took notes, she slipped out of the room, quietly shutting the door behind her. As soon as she was out of T-Mac's sight, she ran down the hallway to the emergency exit. She was outside the embassy and hurrying toward a taxi stand when a vehicle rolled up beside her. She moved out of the way, but the driver swerved closer. As the long dark body of an SUV slid to a stop, the door swung open.

Alex didn't have time to jump back.

A man reached forward, grabbed her from behind and covered her mouth with a cloth.

She fought, but the sweet scent covering her

nose made her so sleepy she couldn't keep her eyes open. Alex was lifted and deposited onto the floorboard of the vehicle, and it sped away into a dark abyss.

Chapter Fourteen

Out of habit, Jake placed his headset in his ear. The team didn't go into any mission without the proper communication equipment. They depended on the ability to talk to one another and share what they were seeing from different angles.

For this mission, Jake was on his own. He wouldn't have backup. His team wasn't there to cover for him. Teamwork was what made the navy SEALs such an incredible force to reckon with. They'd learned in BUD/S training to rely on each other to get through the hard times.

Then why had he insisted on coming alone?

With no time to second-guess his decision, Jake waited for the darkness to cloak the village and make the sentries lazy and sleepy.

As soon as all sunlight had leached from the sky and the stars came out to light his way, Jake made his move. Ducking low, he ran from bush to tree to bush, keeping to the darker shadows and staying out of the open areas as much as possible. Within a few minutes, he was past the sentry he'd been watching and inside the perimeter, and had come to the first mud-and-stick hut.

Moving with the reflexes and stealth of a cat, he crept through the village streets, angling toward the big hut at the center. What he wouldn't give to have some of his buddies providing cover while he moved forward. Their method of leapfrogging forward had saved them on numerous occasions when they'd been surprised by a sniper perched on top of a building.

He'd reached the corner of a smaller hut across from his target when his headset crackled and a voice came over.

"Big Jake, you out there?" a familiar voice asked.

"Harm? That you, buddy?" he whispered.

"Roger," Harm responded. "The gang's all here, minus T-Mac."

Jake tensed. "Alex?"

"T-Mac's pulling guard duty back at the capital."

Jake let go of the breath he'd been holding. He owed T-Mac big-time.

"Where are you?" Harm asked.

"South side of the biggest hut in the village, about to make my move."

"Good. I've got your back. Buck just eliminated one of the guards on the back side of the big hut."

"There are two Tangos at the front door," Jake noted. "I'll take the guy on the right."

"I've got Lefty," Harm said. "On three?"

"On three," Jake agreed.

"One…two…three," Harm counted.

Jake looked both ways, slipped out of his hiding place, sneaked up on the right side of the hut's front and grabbed the man on the right half-dozing against the wall of the building.

At the same time, a shadowy figure came out of seemingly nowhere and snagged the guy on the left. Neither of the sentries had time to cry out before they were dispatched.

Jake eased open the door to the hut. In the limited light from the stars outside, Jake could see a short corridor stretched to the opposite end of the structure. There were doors on each side of the hallway and one at the end.

The doors on the sides had handles but no locks on the exterior. The entry at the other end of the corridor had a latch and a lock securing it on the outside. Jake figured they'd found the missionaries. Who else would they keep locked up? The rest of the villagers seemed to be going about their normal business, maybe short some of their able-bodied men.

Now that they'd found them, getting the missionaries out wouldn't be as quiet as Jake had hoped. But he'd brought along something to help in what he did best—explosives.

He pressed a small wad of C-4 against the hasp, set the detonator into it and backed up to the other doors on the side where Harm waited, his knife drawn.

The two men covered their ears and hunkered down as Jake pressed the button.

A soft version of an explosion sent dust flying, and the lock dropped to the ground.

That was when the fun began.

Men ran out of the two side doors.

Jake and Harm were ready, taking down the first men out on both sides easily. The next ones put up a fight, but were quickly subdued. Their jobs weren't done until they cleared the rooms and checked for any other fighters.

Jake stood to the side of the open door, inhaled deeply and dived through, then rolled across the ground and came up in front of a surprised ISIS rebel holding a rifle.

Jake had moved so quickly, the rebel was still aiming chest-high at the door. As he rose to his feet, Jake caught the weapon and pushed the muzzle toward the ceiling. The rifle went off.

"Shouldn't have done that," Jake said as he jerked the weapon from the man's hands and bashed the butt against the man's face, breaking his nose.

The man went down, and Jake dispatched him with his knife.

"I hope you two are done playing around in there," Diesel's voice came across the headset. "You're going to have company soon. Get out while the going's good. We've cleared a path to the south toward the hills. But you have to move now."

An old man and woman crouched on the floor in the corner of the room, holding each other in their arms.

"Reverend Townsend?" Jake held out a hand.

The old man laid his hand in Jake's. "Yes. That's me."

"Alex sent us. But we have to get you two out of here. Are you able to move on your own?"

"My wife may need a little help, but I can."

"Then let's get out of here." Jake hooked an

arm around Mrs. Townsend and half carried her to the door leading out of the hut, stepping over the ISIS fighters they'd taken out of the running.

"We need cover," Harm said into his headset.

"Gotcha covered," Diesel said. "Go!"

Jake and Harm guided the older couple out of the hut and through the streets of the village.

Gunfire filled the night as Diesel, Buck and Pitbull made it sound as though an entire brigade had descended on the ISIS fighters. They had to move quickly since their supply of ammunition was low and they had a long hike to the SUV.

When Jake and Harm had their charges out of the village and well on their way to the hidden vehicles, Jake let the others know they could abandon the village and make their way to their predetermined rendezvous.

"Get out before they fire up their trucks and flood us with headlights," Jake said into his mic.

A chuckle came over his headset. "Got that covered," Buck's voice chimed in. "Diesel cut their battery cables. They won't be flooding anything but their engines trying to start their vehicles."

Jake loved his team. They thought of everything, and they'd come to back him up on his fool's errand. He couldn't have succeeded without their assistance.

But they weren't out of trouble yet. The reverend and his wife were slow, their old bodies no match for the younger rebels running through the night.

When Buck, Diesel and Pitbull caught up, Pitbull covered their tail while Buck and Diesel wrapped the old man's arms over their shoulders and ran with him.

Mrs. Townsend complained that her arms hurt from being carried in such a manner.

Jake and Harm stopped to regroup.

"I've got this," Jake said. "Sorry, ma'am, but we need to move faster." He tossed the woman over his shoulder and ran toward his SUV.

Darkness was their friend, allowing them to get away without providing clearly visible targets for the rebels. But the rebels were closing in on them. Soon they would be within firing range.

The group split, heading in the direction of their hidden vehicles.

Harm stayed with Jake, offering to carry Mrs. Townsend.

Jake refused the offer, knowing they were

only seconds away from trouble. They couldn't afford to stop again. His lungs burned and his muscles strained against the added weight. But he didn't quit. These people were Americans.

Shots rang out behind them.

Harm turned and fired into the darkness.

And then they were at the SUV.

Harm opened the back door.

Jake dumped Mrs. Townsend onto the seat, and Harm ran around to the driver's side.

By the time Jake slipped into the passenger seat, Harm already had the vehicle in Drive. He blasted through the brush and raced across the bumpy ground, navigating by starlight. He didn't hit the brakes once, knowing the brake and taillights would give the ISIS rebels targets to aim for.

Headlights flared behind them.

"What the hell?" Jake muttered, looking back at two vehicles following them.

"Damn, I must have missed a couple," Diesel said into Jake's headset. "We're closing in on you. You've got the missus?"

Jake glanced back at Mrs. Townsend, who was still trying to buckle her seat belt. Thankfully, she was all right. "We've got Mrs. Townsend. How's the reverend?"

"A trooper," Diesel responded. "Now, if we could only shake this tail."

Harm drove the SUV out onto the dirt road leading back to Niamey. Another vehicle burst from the brush onto the road in front of them. Since it was running without lights, Jake knew it was the one carrying the rest of his team and the reverend.

They sped along the road, picking up speed, but they were at a disadvantage without lights. Several times, the vehicle in front of them skidded sideways to negotiate a turn.

Just when Jake thought they might actually lose the vehicles behind them, brake lights glowed bright red in front of them.

"Why are you slowing down?" Jake asked.

"Watch out. There's a herd of African buffalo lying on the road."

Jake muttered a curse and spun in his seat to watch as the rebel vehicles grew closer. "Honk! Bump them, do something. It's getting hot back here."

"Does no good for us to hit them. They'd put the vehicle out of commission."

The sound of a horn honking ahead might help with the cattle situation, but the oncoming ISIS vehicles weren't slowing one bit and Jake's vehicle was at a complete standstill.

"Pick me up on the other side of the herd," he said and jumped out of the vehicle.

"What the hell?" Harm said as Jake slammed the door.

Diesel was only halfway through the herd and making such slow progress they'd never get through before the ISIS militants closed on them.

Jake ran through the creatures, waving his hands and yelling at the top of his lungs.

One by one, the animals rose to their feet and ambled along the road.

Jake kept running to the other end of the herd and started on his way back, waving, shouting and sometimes shoving the animals out of the way.

The rebel headlights were less than a mile away and closing fast.

Slowly the buffalo woke and started to move a little faster.

Diesel's vehicle cleared the herd and sped away.

Harm pulled up next to Jake.

Jake jumped in, and Harm drove past the rest of the buffalo and picked up speed. But they'd lost a lot of their lead and the buffalo had, for the most part, cleared the road by the time the trailing vehicles reached them.

"Mrs. Townsend, lie low in the seat," Jake said. "We'll likely take some bullets."

She ducked out of the shoulder strap and lay across the seat, her eyes wide.

Within seconds, bullets peppered the back of the SUV, cracking the rear windshield. The bumpy road shook the glass so hard that shards broke loose. Soon the rear window was nothing more than a jagged hole.

Jake climbed over the console and Mrs. Townsend to the rear of the vehicle. He knocked out the glass and, staying below the tailgate, he aimed his rifle at a position just above the right headlight. With the SUV rocking over every rut, he knew his aim would veer off course. He pulled the trigger, firing several rounds.

The lead rebel vehicle swerved sharply to the right, flipped and rolled.

Jake pumped a fist and then braced himself as they hit another deep rut.

The second rebel vehicle slowed only slightly and then raced forward, leaving the other crashed vehicle on the side of the road.

Sitting cross-legged, Jake took aim again. The vehicle was closer. A man hung out of the passenger side firing rounds from a machine gun.

Focusing all of his attention just above the right headlight, Jake fired once, twice, three times.

The vehicle slowed and then jerked to the side. The man hanging out the window pitched forward and fell to the ground. The truck raced to the side and smashed into a tree.

Jake drew in a deep breath and let it out.

"Good job," Harm said. "Now, let's get these good people to Niamey." Harm turned on the lights. Ahead of them, Diesel did, as well.

Jake crawled back into the passenger seat, his heartbeat returning to normal. "That wasn't so bad," he said.

Harm chuckled. "You're just damned lucky we showed up when we did."

"Yeah, yeah. I could have handled it."

Diesel snorted into Jake's ear. "Yeah, right."

Jake knew his team had saved his butt, as well as the Townsends. And they knew he knew. "Thanks, guys."

Fifteen minutes later, they came across another vehicle headed their way, headlights glaring.

When Diesel swerved to the right, the other vehicle swerved in front of him.

Diesel and Harm slammed on their brakes.

Jake jumped out, weapon drawn.

Ahead of him, Buck and Pitbull had done the same, aiming their weapons at the vehicle blocking their way.

The driver in the other vehicle climbed out, his hands in the air. "Hey, it's me, T-Mac. Don't shoot!"

Jake ran toward the other man, his pulse kicking up. "What's wrong? Why are you here? Where's Alex?"

"We have a problem," T-Mac said. "Alex got away. I was hoping she'd found her way to you."

A lead weight settled in Jake's gut. "No, she's not with us. I thought you could handle her."

T-Mac shook his head. "I had a call from the CO. While I was online with him, she snuck out of my room. By the time I realized it, she was gone."

Jake's heart squeezed so hard in his chest he thought it would burst. "Where the hell is she?"

"I went to her room, hoping to find her there."

"And?" Jake snapped.

T-Mac shook his head. "Nothing but a cell phone in the middle of the bed." He dug the device out of his pocket and handed it to Jake.

Jake took it in his hand. It appeared to be a burner phone. He touched the keypad and it lit up.

No Service.

"Damn," Jake cursed. "She didn't have a cell phone on her. Are you sure the maid didn't leave it there?"

"The maid didn't leave it. Someone else did." T-Mac pointed to the phone. "There's a text message."

He pushed the button for the messages, and words appeared on the screen.

Jake's heart sank.

If you want to see the girl, follow the instructions.

He pressed several keys, but no more messages came up on the display. "What damned instructions?"

"We have to assume they'll be coming," T-Mac said.

He'd be waiting. Alex might be gone, but Jake wouldn't give up on her. She wouldn't give up on anyone she cared about.

Neither would Jake. And he really cared about the feisty female he'd met only a few days ago. He cared more than he'd ever cared about a woman before. If he had to go AWOL, he'd keep searching for her until he found her.

Chapter Fifteen

Alex blinked her eyes wide open. Where was she? The seat beside her wasn't part of an elaborate living room set. It was a car seat, and she wasn't on it. She was wedged between it and the backs of more car seats. Based on the bumps and vibrations, she was lying on the floorboard of a moving vehicle.

The windows were dark, indicating it was nighttime. How long had she been unconscious? Was it the same day Jake had left her, or had she slept through to the next night?

Where was she? What happened? Why were her wrists bound with zip ties?

A thousand thoughts raced through her fuzzy head as she shifted to relieve the pressure on her hip. The vehicle she was being transported in hit bumps too often for the road to be one of the Niamey city streets. Dust seeped in through the vents, settling on her skin and every surface.

They were on a dirt road, but where were they going? Did it even matter whether she knew? No one would find her. No one had seen her being taken in the night.

A face appeared between the two front seats—a familiar one. "Ah, Miss Parker, so good of you to join us."

"Philburn," she said, and winced at the pain slicing through her head. She felt like she had a hell of a hangover, but she pushed past the discomfort and the drowsiness threatening to reclaim her, desperate to know what was happening to her. "Where are we?"

"We're out in the godforsaken hills of Niger. You will likely recognize some of the landmarks along the way, as you and your navy SEAL boyfriend traveled this route recently."

"You're taking me to the mine?" she asked, attempting to pull herself up onto the seat and failing with each successive bump.

"I'm taking you to the test site. We aren't mining yet. That would be presumptuous of us when we haven't received government clearance to mine yet."

"In other words, you jumped the legal gun and started without government approval," she stated, wishing her head didn't hurt so badly and that she could push up to a sitting position. Every bump jolted her back and made the muscles in her body tense up.

"Only a formality," Philburn said.

"In the meantime, you're mining materials you aren't reporting to the Niger government."

"Not mining. Testing," he corrected.

"I see. And anyone who says differently will be silenced?" she asked, knowing the answer. A shiver shook her frame, but she refused to let him see that she was afraid.

Philburn's lip curled. "You're smarter than I gave you credit for."

"And the ISIS raid on my village?"

"Takes the heat off my operation and provides me with fresh workers." He smirked. "A killer combination."

"I'm surprised the Niger government hasn't caught on to you yet. Surely word gets around."

He snorted. "Only if you let it."

Based on the angle of the vehicle and the strain on the engine, they were climbing.

Whatever Philburn had drugged her with still pulled at her, making her drowsy. She drifted in and out of consciousness. Each time she came to, her mind was a little clearer and her throat more parched, dust filling her nostrils.

After what seemed like an eternity, the driver pulled the vehicle to a stop and switched off the engine.

Alex opened her eyes and noted the sky out the window had lightened into the dull gray of predawn.

Seconds later, another engine roared to life and wheels rumbled over the gravel near where they were parked.

Philburn exited the SUV and slammed the door. The driver climbed out and opened the rear door. "What do you want me to do with her?" he asked over the top of the roof.

"Take her to my office and secure her there," Philburn said.

His driver grabbed Alex beneath her shoulders, hauled her out of the vehicle, stood her on her feet and bent to toss her over his shoulder.

Alex brought her knee up hard, smashing it into the man's nose.

He fell to his knees, pressing his hand to his face.

Alex swiveled around in a sidekick, catching him in the temple. He went down and lay still.

With no plan in mind, only a loose-baked idea, Alex ran back down the hill they'd just climbed in the SUV.

Shouts sounded behind her, but she kept

running, her hands bound at her back. If she could make it into the brush, she might have a chance of losing her pursuers.

Footsteps pounded in the gravel, closing in on her.

Drawing on her years of racing on the high school track team, she pushed harder, ran faster and ducked into the brush.

She'd run hurdles higher than the bramble and limbs she cleared, but she didn't have her arms free to balance her landings. On her first leap, she made it over the bush, landed, stumbled and righted herself. Alex charged forward, trying her hardest to put distance between her and the guards following her.

Just when she thought she might have a chance, she flew over the top of a bush and landed on the other side in a small rut. Small by the road's standards, but deep enough to twist her ankle. She went down hard. When she tried to stand, pain shot up her leg.

Alex rolled into the bush and lay still, praying the guards would run right past her without seeing her lying on the ground.

She focused on controlling her heavy breathing, wiggled herself into the dried leaves and brush, and willed herself to become the smallest, most easily ignored lump of human being she could be.

The first guard ran past her. The second one slowed and walked by. The third stopped directly in front of the bush where she lay.

"Do you see her?" shouted the first guard.

"No. She was here a moment ago," the second one answered.

"Maybe she's hiding," the third guard said, and glanced down at his feet.

Why couldn't he have asked that question *after* he'd passed her? Alex didn't dare to breathe or move even an eyelash.

The three guards stopped running and glanced around the area, pushing branches aside, kicking at clumps of grass.

The one in front of her used his foot to push aside a low-hanging branch. The toe of his boot brushed against Alex's side.

She swallowed the gasp rising up her throat, her muscles tensing.

"She's here!" the guard shouted, and lunged for her.

Alex pushed to her knees and threw herself forward, half running, half limping, but not moving fast enough to get away.

The three guards surrounded her.

She glared at them. "What you are doing is

illegal. You will go to jail when you're caught. Let me go and I'll see to it you are free."

None of them were deterred by her threat.

One darted forward.

Alex swung her injured foot out, caught the man in the chest and shoved him backward. Pain reverberated through her ankle, calf and thigh.

The other two pounced, grabbed her beneath her arms and legs, and lifted her off the ground.

She fought and kicked like a wild animal, but they were stronger and managed to carry her back up the hill to the mining compound.

Quinten Philburn waited with his arms crossed over his chest. "Do that again, and I'll authorize them to kill you." He jerked his head to the side. "Put her in my office, bind her and don't let her escape again, or I'll have you shot."

That was when Alex realized there would be no reasoning with the guards at the camp. They worked for Philburn. And if they didn't do what he said, he'd have them killed. Nice management philosophy, and, based on the number of guards and the number of men working the mine, it worked for him.

Her chances of escaping the compound looked pretty slim. Still, she wasn't giving up yet.

As the guards carried her into a small portable office made from a metal shipping container, she studied her surroundings, searching for something she could use to cut the zip ties they'd applied to her wrists and the one they secured around her ankles. If she could free her hands and feet, she might have another chance of escaping. She'd have to wait until dark and sneak out of the camp. Running in daylight gave her pursuers all the advantages. And this time, they wouldn't run after her. They'd just shoot.

She waited until the men left the building before she put her plan into place. All the while she worked at her bindings, she wondered if Jake had found the Townsends. And if he had, had he been able to get them away from their ISIS captors? Mostly, she wanted to know if he had survived.

Her heart squeezed hard in her chest. She prayed he was okay and that she would see him again soon. His kisses were heaven, and making love to him… Well, he was the kind of man dreams were made of. If she got a second chance, she'd tell him how she felt, even if it seemed silly after only a short time. And if he didn't reciprocate those feelings—oh, well. By putting herself and her feelings out there, she would have at least tried.

"CAN YOU GO any faster?" Jake demanded.

"I've got my foot to the floor and we barely made the last curve in the road without flipping this vehicle." Harm held his white-knuckle grip on the steering wheel as he maneuvered around another sharp curve in the road. "What more do you want?"

"I want to get to some place with cell phone reception." He shook the hand holding the burner phone in the air. "We have no other way to find Alex. This damned phone and the ability to receive messages could mean life or death for her."

The sun had yet to rise, and the predawn sky barely gave enough light to avoid obstructions in the road until they were practically on them. Twice Harm had to slam on the breaks to avoid hitting a large animal. After the buffalo herd, they'd come across a giraffe standing in the middle of the lane, munching on the leaves of a tree hanging over the road. At another spot, they'd almost run over a pack of hyenas fighting over a carcass. They were almost all the way back to Niamey before they regained cell phone reception.

The phone in Jake's hand buzzed with an incoming text message. He nearly dropped the device in his hurry to read the message.

While Harm kept driving toward the embassy, Jake read aloud: Jake Schuler, if you want the girl meet me at these coordinates at midnight alone, or she dies.

The coordinates were listed after the words.

"You can't go alone," Harm said.

Jake shook his head. "I can't risk taking anyone with me."

"We'll make a plan." Harm shot a glance toward him. "Hell, he's giving you all day to come up with something."

Jake frowned, staring at the text as if he might glean more information than was written on the screen. "Why did he set the meeting at midnight?"

"He's hiding," Harm said.

Jake clutched the phone in his fist, his heart racing, his desire to act making him edgy. "I say we go now."

"No way. If you go now, you'll be seen from miles away. We need to look at the map, see where exactly he's taking you." Harm sped through the streets of Niamey and pulled up to the gate at the embassy. "We need to let T-Mac do his computer thing and see if he can determine who sent that text. That might give us more of a clue who we're up against."

Harm spoke with the gate guard and waited for the guard to call for clearance to allow them to bring Reverend and Mrs. Townsend into the complex.

While the guards checked both vehicles for explosive devices, Jake tapped his fingers on the armrest, counting the seconds until they could get to their rooms and devise a plan.

Finally they were cleared to enter.

Harm shifted into Drive and continued their conversation as if it hadn't been interrupted for ten minutes. "While T-Mac's doing the computer work, we can get online with the CO and see if we can get some support for this operation." He glanced in the rearview mirror and smiled. "Good morning, Mrs. Townsend." Harm glanced over to Jake. "We couldn't have left immediately, anyway. We had passengers who needed to be delivered to safety."

Jake knew Harm was right on all counts, but it didn't make him feel any better. Every fiber of his being physically ached to be on the road to the coordinates listed in the text. He couldn't imagine what horrors Alex might be experiencing at that moment. But he knew Harm was right. His most recent solo experience had taught him a valuable lesson. He needed the support of his team. The more support he had, the better chance he had of rescuing Alex.

The SUVs were met at the front of the complex. An ambulance was on standby to transport the Townsends to the nearest hospital for medical care and evaluation.

Ambassador Brightbill insisted on a debriefing immediately and attended with the missionaries and the SEAL team.

Jake and his teammates filed into the conference room following the Townsends. The Townsends gave their statement and were cleared to leave in the waiting ambulance.

When they'd left the room, Ambassador Brightbill addressed the SEALs, his brow furrowed. "You realize you conducted an unsanctioned operation in this country, and I will have to answer to the repercussions, don't you?"

Jake stood tall and proud, refusing to take any kind of flak from some desk jockey of a politician. "Yes, sir."

The ambassador narrowed his eyes and stared at each SEAL one at a time. Then his frown lifted. "Thank you. I doubt I could have gotten as quick a response had I gone through the proper channels to get help. If you need anything, just ask me. Thomas, my executive officer, had a family emergency come up and had to leave Niger to return to the States on short notice, or he would have been at this debrief with me." He stood and shook hands with each of the men. "Thank you for all you do for our country and our people."

Shocked by the show of support, Jake shook the man's hand. "If you'll excuse us, we'd like to get cleaned up," he lied. To protect the ambassador as much as to protect Alex, Jake didn't enlighten Brightbill on the next non-sanctioned operation they would be conducting that night.

He found it better to ask for forgiveness than permission. Ambassador Brightbill would understand.

The team hurried to T-Mac's room. He brought up the borrowed laptop, keyed in the coordinates and zoomed in on the map.

Buck leaned over T-Mac's chair. "That's out in the middle of nowhere."

"The story of our tour in Africa," Diesel muttered. "At least it's not on the Congo River with gorillas and crocodiles."

"Yeah, but there could be hungry lions, or angry rhinoceroses," Pitbull said.

"Just so you know," T-Mac said. "While you all were out playing heroes and bad guys getting the Townsends out of that village, I made a deal with the devil."

"You called the commander." Hope swelled inside Jake. "And?"

"He thought things were hot enough around here to send reinforcements. Two more helicopters from the 160th Night Stalkers should be landing at the Special Forces location near us within the hour, where the previous helicopter is still waiting. The two additional choppers are coming complete with another twelve of our closest friends."

Jake grabbed T-Mac's shoulders from behind. "I could kiss you."

T-Mac held up his hands. "Save it for someone who wants it, dude. I'm not your type. But there's more."

"More?" Jake stared at T-Mac's reflection in the computer screen. "As if reinforcements weren't enough?"

T-Mac grinned. "He also sent the drone to conduct recon missions and provide additional firepower, should we need it. Give me a minute and I'll find out the status of both and convey the coordinates for a high flyover reconnaissance mission by the drone."

"As long as it doesn't alert the kidnapper that we're on to them."

"Got it." T-Mac bent to the computer and placed a video call to their commander back in Djibouti.

The CO responded in seconds. "You better be calling to say you found our AWOL SEAL."

Jake leaned down to get his face in view of the camera. "Sir, I'm here."

"Any casualties?" the commander barked.

"Not on our end, sir," Jake responded.

"If not on our end, then whose end?" their boss asked.

"Let's just say some of the ISIS folks who crashed our party a couple days ago won't be bothering us again."

"Good." The commander's eyes narrowed. "So, am I correct in assuming I can send a C-17 aircraft to pick up my choppers and drone and expect you six troublemakers back in Djibouti with them?"

Jake ran a hand through his hair. "Well, sir, about that."

His commander's lips thinned and his jaw

tightened until there was a tick twitching on one side of his face. "What now?"

"You remember that teacher I helped escape the ISIS attack on that village?" Jake asked.

"The one who insisted you go after the reverend and his wife?" The CO nodded. "What about her?"

"She was kidnapped last night."

The commander scrubbed a hand over his face and then stared at him from the screen. "I guess it doesn't make a difference if I tell you it's not your problem."

"Sir, no sir. It is my problem. If I don't agree to meet with them, they'll kill her."

"And how do you know they want *you* to meet with them, and not someone else?"

Jake sighed. "The text message had my name on it."

The commander nodded, his lips twisting. "Which makes it your problem."

"Yes, sir."

The CO scrubbed a hand over his face again. "You know I can't authorize you to go in alone."

Jake straightened, his fists clenched at his sides. "No disrespect, sir, but I'm going."

His commander waved a hand. "That's a

given. I'm sure if I told you that you couldn't, you'd go AWOL again."

As a man who valued his career as a navy SEAL, Jake knew what that could mean. But it didn't matter. Alex was out there, being threatened and possibly tortured. "Yes, sir. I'd go anyway."

The CO tapped a pen against his desk for a moment and then glanced up. "Okay, then, but you'll do it my way, or I withdraw my birds. Got it?"

Jake scowled. "But sir, I have to go in alone, or he'll kill her."

"Did I say you weren't going in alone?" The older SEAL cocked an eyebrow.

"No, sir," Jake said.

"Then listen up." The CO looked past Jake. "And that goes for the rest of your team. Are they there? Can they hear me?"

"Yes, sir!" All six men gathered around the computer while their commander told them the game plan and how the helicopters and drone would play a part. When he was done talking, he signed off and the men put his plan into action.

Jake prayed they were in time, and that whoever was holding Alex wouldn't get nervous and kill her anyway.

He figured it was time to go to work, doing what SEALs do best.

Chapter Sixteen

With what little light came through the small window of the cargo container office, Alex searched for anything rough enough to help her break her bonds.

When she couldn't find a coarse edge, she made one by smashing the leg off a wooden chair and using the jagged, splintered end to scrape the plastic tie across. She held the broken wooden stake between her fingers and ran the plastic over the broken leg again and again.

A couple times she scraped the skin on her wrists, causing them to bleed. Ignoring the pain, she worked harder, determined to get herself out of the mess she was in.

No matter how hard she scraped, the zip tie didn't break. With her wrists bound behind her back and ankles locked together, she couldn't get very far.

After several hours' work at her bindings,

the heat in the office bore down on her. Sweat dripped into her eyes, making them burn. Despair threatened to take hold and suck her under.

Each time she got the feeling all was lost, she'd remember how wonderful it had felt to make love with Jake. The images conjured up made her all the more determined to get free and see the man again, even if only for a minute, an hour or a day. She didn't try to think beyond that because he was a SEAL and she was a teacher. It wasn't as if they could have a future together. Heck, they barely knew each other. He probably didn't want the burden of a relationship anyway.

But she wouldn't know if she didn't try. And she'd never wanted to try more than she did at that moment. Jake was worth the effort.

When the broken chair leg didn't make much of a dent in the hard plastic bindings, Alex looked around the room for anything else.

In one corner of the office lay a metal ammunition box. If she could get it open, the edge of the box might be strong enough that she could rub the plastic tie over it until it broke.

Alex inched across the floor, turned her back to the box and fumbled with the latch. After a few attempts, she managed to open the ammo box, unhooking and then flipping up the metal clamp.

Inside the box were rifle magazines and bullets. She ignored the contents and rubbed the zip tie along the side edges of the container.

The metal was just coarse enough to impact the integrity of the plastic. When she was well through the density of the plastic and on her way to breaking the tie, the door to the shipping container office jerked open. Bright sunlight blinded Alex for a moment. Fresh warm air wafted into her prison, along with a haze of dust.

Alex sat up straight, pushing the ammo box behind her, out of sight. She blinked up as Quinten Philburn entered the office and smirked down at her.

The man laughed. "Not so cocky now, are you?"

Remembering her father's words that the best defense was a good offense, Alex faced Philburn. "I don't know what you're trying to accomplish, but you're doing it with the wrong person."

He laughed. "I'd say I caught a valuable little prize in you."

"I don't know what you're talking about," she said. "I'm just a teacher. I don't have rich parents. I'm not worth anything to you or any-one else. So why keep me?"

"Oh, but you are worth more than you think. You're going to buy me time."

"Time?"

"Time to clean up and clear out." Philburn waved a hand to the side. "All I have to do is collect a few of the loose ends you and your boyfriend created."

Alex frowned. "I don't understand."

"You will, soon enough." He glanced around the small space. "Any last requests before I leave you?"

"I'd say a steak dinner with a baked potato and a salad, but right now, water would be nice," she said, her voice gravelly, her throat parched in the heat.

Philburn snorted. "I can spare a little water to keep my prize alive a little longer." He gave her one last look and then left the building, closing the door sharply behind him.

Anger burned low in Alex's belly. If she got free, she'd take Philburn down any way she could. The man was the devil.

A moment later, the door burst open again. This time, a guard dressed in a dusty olive-green uniform stood in the door frame, his rifle pointing in at Alex. His glanced around the interior of the office and then stepped back.

A man Alex barely recognized entered, carrying a bucket of water and a dipper. His dark hair, skin and clothing covered in dust, he walked with a limp, and appeared to be much older than she knew him to be.

"Fariji," she gasped. This man, her classroom assistant, was one of the sweetest, kindest men in her village. Alex's heart broke when she spied what appeared to be whip marks across the back of his neck. "What are you doing here?"

With his gaze downcast, he answered, "Miss Alex, I brought you water." Then he bent to hold the dipper to her lips.

Alex drank, filling her dry mouth with the tepid water. So what if it wasn't purified? She'd die of heat exhaustion without it. She swallowed and asked, "Is Philburn forcing you to work his mine?"

Fariji didn't answer but held the dipper to her lips again. Something fell into her lap. For a moment, his gaze met hers, and then his eyelids lowered and he backed slowly away.

Alex drew her knees up, hiding whatever Fariji had purposely dropped.

"Out!" the guard barked at Fariji.

The gentle, sweet man turned and hurried out of the office.

The guard glared back in at Alex and then slammed the door shut.

Footsteps sounded, fading away.

When Alex was certain the guard was gone and wouldn't suddenly reopen the door, she looked down at the article Fariji had left in her lap.

It was a small steel file, probably from a toolbox of one of the workers at the mine.

Alex rolled over, letting it drop to the floor, then scooted around to grab it with her hands behind her back.

Once she had it between her fingers, she sawed at the zip tie. A couple minutes later, the tie snapped and her wrists were free.

A quick rush of joy spread through her, but she refused to bask in it. She had a lot to do before dark, and she prayed Philburn wouldn't return in the meantime. If he caught her without bonds, he'd just have her restrained again and she'd have to start all over.

With her hands free, she made quick work of breaking the zip tie at her ankles. Once she could move around, she searched the drawers, boxes and containers for anything she could use for a weapon. Alas, she had only the metal file.

She tried the door and discovered it was locked from the outside. The window was small, but if she worked at it, she might get through. Not in the daylight, though. Careful not to let anyone see her, she peered through the window and studied what she could see of the compound.

Big trucks carried massive amounts of dirt from the mine, dumping it in piles near something that appeared to be a sifter.

Workers carried buckets of material on their heads or dragged huge sacks behind them.

Guards carried either rifles or whips or both. When a worker fell or stumbled with his load, a guard was right on top of him, yelling or cracking a whip.

She managed to open the window slightly to let in fresh air, though it did little to reduce the increasing temperature inside the cramped container. If Philburn didn't kill her, the heat might.

With little else to do, Alex sat beneath the window and waited for dusk and a chance to escape. When she was free, she'd make her way back to Niamey and demand the Niger government do something about the illegal mining, and that they free the conscripted workers. She wouldn't leave Fariji or any of the others behind. The lies, the torture and forced labor had to come to an end. Good people like Fariji didn't deserve to be abused in this manner.

The heat drained her, but she held tight to hope and the eventual setting of the brutal sun. When the shadows lengthened and light faded from the small window, the unbearable heat lessened and Alex pushed to her feet. It would soon be time to make good her escape.

THROUGHOUT THE MORNING, the SEALs prepared their plan of action. They coordinated with the Special Forces in a nearby camp for helicopter transportation, weapons and ammunition. The SEALs would secure a vehicle and meet up with the rest of the SEAL team that had arrived from Djibouti early that morning.

Their commander had the drone up in the air all morning long, scouting and taking digital pictures of the area surrounding the coordinates given, expanding its surveillance to include several miles around the location.

As soon as the drone completed its survey, the images were transmitted to Military Intelligence back at Djibouti. Within a couple of hours, several pictures were sent to T-Mac, and he downloaded them onto the laptop.

Jake and the others hovered over the man's shoulders as they studied the images, zooming in on one in particular.

"That's the mine we came across when we were in the hills," Jake said. "Do you think Quinten Philburn might have taken Alex?"

"If he's worried you two might report him, he might have," Harm said. "You're the only two outside his organization who've put eyes on his operation."

Jake's body tensed. Deep down, he felt this was where they'd find Alex. "We can't wait until midnight. We need to go sooner. I'd bet my last dollar she's there."

"How can you be so sure?" Buck asked.

"My gut tells me it's so." His belly knotted as if in agreement.

A bell pinged on T-Mac's computer. He switched from the images to a screen full of data. T-Mac bent to examine the information.

Harm shook his head. "Big Jake, we can't base an entire operation just on your gut."

"There's something else." T-Mac held up a hand, his gaze still on the screen in front of him. "When I was looking into Snyder Mining Enterprises, and I found that they were owned by Transunion Mining Corporation and then sold to Colorado Holding Company based out of the Cayman Islands, I couldn't get much information out of them."

"So," Jake prompted.

"I also dug into Thomas Whitley's background. I verified that he did work for Ambassador Brightbill when they both were employed by a company whose subsidiary was Transunion Mining Corporation."

Jake fidgeted, too anxious about Alex to take in a long explanation. "What's your point?" he snapped.

"I found where Whitley had significant shares in Transunion. When it sold, he invested in another corporation." T-Mac glanced up into Jake's eyes. "Colorado Holding Company."

"Whitley?" Jake struggled to digest what T-Mac was telling him. "You think Whitley has a stake in that mining operation? Why didn't you say anything earlier?"

"I was running a program, searching for data on Whitley while we were waiting for the drone images. It finished, and that's what I found." He moved to the side so the others could see the screen.

"We need to talk with the ambassador," Harm said.

"Forget the ambassador," Jake said. "We need to get to the mine."

"One more thing…" T-Mac switched the screen back to the images and zoomed in on the coordinates Jake had been given for the rendezvous. "I wasn't sure when we looked a minute before, but if you peer closer, those aren't the tops of trees down there. Those are camouflage nets." He pointed to the spot on the map. "And if you look here, that's not a tree trunk but a man standing there." He zoomed closer, the image getting grainier. "And he's wearing black and holding a rifle."

"An ISIS fighter," Jake said. "The coordinates are a setup. They want us to go there, knowing I wouldn't go alone. It's a distraction to keep us from finding Alex."

"And to get us all killed," Diesel concluded.

"What if Alex is being held there?" Pitbull asked.

"She's not," Jake said with certainty.

Harm's lips pressed into a line. "But if you're wrong?"

"We plan our operation for just after sundown," Jake said. "If we come up short of Alex, we move to the coordinates indicated in the text message."

Harm, Buck, Diesel, T-Mac and Pitbull nodded and replied, "Agreed."

T-Mac placed a video call to their commander. Jake filled him in on what was happening, and they received his agreement and commitment to support their altered plan.

"We only have a few hours until sundown." Jake started for the door. "Let's get to the Spec Ops camp and meet up with the rest of the team. We need to brief them and ramp up."

They borrowed one of the battered vehicles they'd turned in earlier to the embassy motor pool. In less than fifteen minutes, they were racing out of Niamey into the countryside, headed for the camp where they'd meet up with the rest of the SEAL team their CO had sent to help.

Jake counted the passing seconds, wishing they could have had the team pick them up at the airport and helicopter them out of Niamey. They could have been at the Spec Ops camp in less than an hour. As it was, they would be on the road for well over an hour and a half. He wanted to be there already, and in the air, on the way to find Alex. The minutes went by as if in slow motion.

When they finally pulled into the camp, the place was a hive of activity. Jake, Harm, Diesel, Buck, T-Mac and Pitbull met in the ops tent with the rest of their team from Djibouti and the army Special Forces trainers from the camp and laid out the plan.

The Special Forces guys offered to take the Niger counterparts they'd been training, pre-position them near the rendezvous coordinates and then wait until they received word from the SEAL team before moving in. With or without the SEALs, they were prepared to take out the ISIS fighters they suspected were hiding under the camouflage netting.

With a contingent of eighteen SEALs, three Black Hawk helicopters and enough firepower to take down all of the ISIS militants who'd surprised them less than a week before, they were trained and ready for the mission.

They had everything they needed to get in, take care of business and get out. Now all they had to do was wait until just before sundown. The flight would take less than an hour. They'd fast rope down a couple miles from the mine and go in on foot. They would be there a few hours before the midnight deadline given for the other coordinates.

The hours ticked by slowly. Finally the SEALs loaded into the Black Hawks, the Special Forces team filled trucks and Humvees, and they took off.

Jake's pulse hummed a steady beat as he settled into "go" mode. He channeled all of his energy and focus on the task ahead: rescuing Alex.

Dusk cloaked the land as the helicopters skimmed the treetops and buzzed over herds of wild animals grazing on the grass and brush.

Jake checked and double-checked his weapons, from his HK416 assault rifle with the ten-inch barrel and suppressor to his Sig Sauer P226 handgun. He patted the Ka-Bar knife on his hip and the many extra magazines filled with ammo tucked into the straps on his bulletproof vest.

"Here we go," Harm said as the helicopter slowed to hover over an open patch of hillside a couple miles away from the mining compound. He was first out, fast roping to the ground.

Jake followed, then Buck and the rest of the team.

The other two helicopters hovered nearby, the men slipping to the ground like ghosts in the gloom.

Once on the ground, Jake tapped his headset. "Comm check."

One by one the team checked in, until all eighteen of the SEALs were accounted for.

"Let's do this," Jake said, and took point, leading the men up and over the first ridge. From the top, he could see lights glowing in the distance. Based on the direction, he bet they were coming from the mine. Although why they'd be running at night was beyond him. Then he noticed they weren't lights, but flames rising into the sky.

"You see that?" Jake said into his mic.

Harm came to a halt beside him and took in the scene. "Not a good sign. Let's get there." He dropped over the ridge and ran down the hill.

Jake was on his heels and easily overtook him on the way up the next rise. His calm, professional perspective had taken a hit when he'd seen the flames. He had to get to Alex. Fast.

Chapter Seventeen

At dusk, Alex checked out the window. Men seemed to be working feverishly. But something was different about what was happening. Instead of bringing the dirt and minerals out of the mine, bulldozers were pushing them back into the hole. Men were throwing boxes, shovels, picks and anything that wasn't nailed down into the pit, as well. The displaced brush and trees that had been uprooted to make room for the mining pit were pushed in on top of everything else.

What the hell was going on?

As she watched, the guards herded the dusty, dirty, barefoot men up to the edge of the pit. Several of them had jugs in their hands. They spilled the contents into the pit over the trees and brush. One of the guards lifted a tank with a hose on it and lit a match in front of it. Then he aimed the hose at the pit and blasted a red, blue and orange stream of flame at the debris. The flame caught the accelerant and flashed into the darkening sky.

Alex stood, transfixed by the rising flames, her heart racing.

They were destroying the mine.

Then the guards standing behind the conscripted workers took another step backward and raised their weapons.

"No, they wouldn't," Alex whispered, her pulse leaping and a lead weight dropping in her gut. She scrambled up onto the stack of boxes she'd pushed up against the wall beneath the tiny window. She was desperate to get through the window before the horror began. She had to stop them from killing the workers and dumping them into the pit of flames.

She pushed the narrow rectangular window up as far as the little hinge would take it. Then she turned her head sideways and pushed it through the opening.

A guard was just disappearing around the end of the container box, pouring liquid on the side of it from what appeared to be a gasoline jug. The pungent scent of gas burned Alex's nostrils. Then a flame blasted around the corner from the direction the guard had gone and raced toward her.

Alex ducked her head back in, panic threatening to overwhelm her. They were lighting the container box on fire with her in it. What happened to using her as bait? What kind of bait would she be if she was dead?

With renewed determination, Alex poked her head out of the shipping container office again and stared down at the fire licking up the side of the metal box. Surely it wouldn't do anything to the box but burn the paint off the exterior. Whoever had poured the gasoline had forgotten the box was made of metal.

Smoke rose from the grass around the box, filling her lungs and making her eyes sting. The box itself might not burn, but Alex had to get out before the smoke and heat consumed her. She pushed her arms and head through the opening and then shimmied her body halfway through.

Near the edge of the mine, the guards stood with their weapons raised as if waiting for a signal from someone.

Two men strode up to one of the guards.

One was Philburn. Alex could tell by the man's annoying swagger. The other was Whitley, the US ambassador's executive officer. They must have given the guard instructions because he walked back to the other guards watching over the workers. Meanwhile Philburn and Whitley moved in the opposite direction, heading for a leveled patch of ground where a helicopter waited.

Anger burned inside Alex, fueling her determination to free herself from the tomb of a box they intended her to die in.

Once the gasoline had been consumed, the fire around the box died down. The rumble of heavy machinery starting up sounded nearby, followed by the clanking of a tracked vehicle moving. The shipping container office lurched, jolting as if it had been hit hard from behind. The force jerked her body and made her flap against the side of the container like a rag doll. Someone was pushing the container toward the pit.

Alex had two choices: get out or die. She wiggled and shoved her way through, the window's edge catching on her hips as she hung halfway out.

With all attention focused on the guards holding the guns on the workers, no one seemed to be watching the container. The office building moved ever closer to the pit, picking up speed as it slid across the uneven ground.

Alex grunted and cursed as she pushed and

pulled herself as far as she could, until she could move no more. She needed help.

A shadowy figure ran in front of her.

Alex swallowed a yelp. Fariji grabbed her shoulders, braced his feet against the side of the box and pulled as hard as he could. Alex barely moved.

"I'm stuck," she said. "You have to go, Fariji," she begged. "Save yourself."

"I won't go without you, Miss Alex." Walking backward as the container moved closer and closer to the pit, Fariji planted his feet on the side of the box and pulled again.

This time, her hips slipped past the window frame and she fell to the ground on top of Fariji. They rolled sideways, away from the oncoming structure. They couldn't seem to move fast enough to get to the other end. Fariji grabbed Alex's arm and leaped out of the way, pulling her with him as the container was pushed over the edge and crashed into the mining pit.

"You just can't leave well enough alone, can you, Miss Parker?" Quinten Philburn stepped out of the darkness, a handgun pointed at Alex's chest.

Fariji still held on to her arm.

"We don't have time to deal with them," Whitley said, and turned away. "Shoot them." And he left his partner and walked toward the waiting helicopter.

When Philburn shifted the barrel of the pistol toward Fariji, Alex reacted.

She swung her leg out, hitting Philburn's hand.

The gun went off, but the bullet went wide instead of hitting Fariji in the chest.

Without giving the man the chance to aim again, Alex grabbed his wrist with both hands. "Run, Fariji!"

Her friend didn't move. "I won't leave without you, Miss Alex."

Philburn wrestled Alex for control of the handgun, his greater strength moving it to between the two of them and pressing it to her belly. When Fariji lunged forward, Philburn yelled, "Back off, or I'll kill her."

Fariji raised his hands and stepped back. "Don't kill Miss Alex. She's a good person."

Philburn snorted. "I've had more than enough of you, Alexandria Parker. Your interference has cost me too much."

"You're a cold, heartless bastard. You deserve all the bad juju you get." Alex stared into the man's face and spit in his eye. She closed her own and braced herself for when the gun went off.

JAKE REACHED THE edge of the camp first, running full on to get to Alex before something awful happened. The flames leaped high into the air, lighting the area in and around the mining pit. Dark silhouettes stood out against the bright blaze—men standing by the pit, other men carrying weapons, a commercial helicopter nearby.

"There!" Harm pointed toward a woman with long hair struggling with a man who had something in his hand. A gun?

Jake raced toward them, anger, fear and adrenaline pushing him faster. He came up behind the man and attempted to jerk him free of Alex. As he did so, the loud crack of a gun made him flinch and his heart come to a complete stop.

"Alex?" he cried, staring at her in the glow of the fire.

"I'm okay," she said, her voice strained as she held on to the man's wrists with both hands to keep him from shooting her.

Running on instinct, Jake knocked the

weapon out of the man's hand and flung him to the ground.

The man beneath him was Quinten Philburn.

Alex grabbed the gun and took off.

"Where are you going?" Jake asked.

"To stop them from shooting the workers." She waved toward the helicopter. "Don't let that chopper get off the ground!" she yelled, heading toward the group of men near the lip of the pit.

"Harm, take over here." Jake leaped to his feet and raced after Alex. Was she insane? One woman with a handgun against a dozen men equipped with semiautomatic rifles didn't bode well. "I could use some help near the pit," he said into his mic.

"We see the problem," Diesel responded, "and we're right behind you."

"Good." Jake caught Alex around the waist and yanked her back from tearing after the guards.

The SEAL team overtook Alex and Jake and raced toward the guards who had raised their weapons to their shoulders like executioners.

Diesel, Pitbull, Buck and T-Mac pointed their rifles into the air, fired and whooped like wild men.

The guards jerked around, saw the SEALs

running straight for them and freaked out. Half of them threw down their weapons and ran. The other half turned on the SEALs, pointing their weapons at the charging fighters.

Before the guards could fire, the team dropped to their knees and unloaded their magazines on Quinten's men fighting back, careful not to hit the unarmed men who'd been held captive to work the mines.

Alex struggled in Jake's arms. "We have to stop that helicopter," she said, then wiggled free of Jake's hold and took off in the opposite direction toward the chopper as the rotors began to turn.

Jake caught up to her. "Is Whitley on board?"

"Yes," she said, racing across the uneven terrain.

"Stay back and let me handle it." Jake sprinted ahead, leaving her behind as he ran toward the chopper. The wind whipped up by the helicopter blades fanned the flames in the pit, making them leap and spit giant flakes of hot ash and soot.

As Jake reached the aircraft, it lifted off the ground.

He dived for the open door.

Whitley slammed it shut.

Jake fell over the skid, hooked his arm

around the metal runner and held on as the helicopter rose higher into the air. He pulled himself up until he was standing on the skid. Then he yanked open the door, grabbed Whitley around the throat in a headlock the man couldn't break and pressed his P226 handgun against Whitley's temple.

"Put this aircraft on the ground!" he shouted to the pilot.

When the pilot hesitated, Jake redirected his aim and fired a shot through the door next to the pilot. "Now!"

The pilot adjusted the helicopter flight controls suddenly, tilting the craft toward Jake in an attempt to throw him off the skid.

Jake held on to Whitley's neck. The safety harness securing Whitley in the aircraft held both men.

Whitley clawed at the arm around his neck, but couldn't break Jake's stronghold.

"I'm not going anywhere, and the next bullet will be in you!" Jake shouted above the roar of the spinning rotors. "And to hell with landing this bird. Crash it, and I crash with you." He pointed the pistol at the pilot. "Go ahead. Try me."

"For the love of God," Whitley wheezed into his headset. "Put it down."

The pilot looked from Whitley to Jake and back, and then maneuvered the helicopter back over the trees toward the mining pit now spewing flames high into the sky.

As they neared the clear pad from which they'd taken off, the wind shifted suddenly and the smoke and flames blew toward the helicopter, engulfing them in a thick, acrid cloud.

Jake's eyes stung and his throat tightened as he inhaled a big gulp of smoke. He blinked and glanced down through a sudden break in the smoke and noted the ground only ten feet from the bottom of the skid on which he stood.

Not willing to take a chance on the pilot's ability to fly or land the chopper in blackout conditions, Jake made a split-second decision and took a chance. He released Whitley's neck and dropped out of the helicopter.

ALEX STOOD TRANSFIXED, her heart squeezing hard in her chest as she watched the drama unfold.

She nearly had a heart attack when Jake leaped onto the helicopter. And how he held on to the side of the aircraft was nothing short of phenomenal. How he would get down without falling back to the earth would need another miracle.

She held her breath, praying out loud, "Please, let him be okay. Please, let him come down in one piece. Oh, God, let Jake be all right."

Harm raced over to her.

"What happened to Philburn?" she asked.

"Zip-tied and gagged. I have one of the guys standing watch over him." He looked around. "Where's Jake?"

Alex swallowed hard and pointed up at the helicopter.

Harm squinted up into the night. The blaze gave just enough light that they could see the silhouette of a man hanging on to the outside of the chopper.

"Tell me that's not Jake," Harm muttered.

"I wish I could." She stared up at the sky, her body trembling, tears stinging her eyes. "What was he thinking?"

"That's Jake for you. He doesn't like leaving loose ends." Harm shook his head. "Damned fool. What am I supposed to tell the CO if I have to bring him back in a body bag?"

Alex gasped and tears spilled from her eyes.

Harm glanced down. "Sorry. If I know Jake, he'll find a way out of this. That man's always coming up smelling like roses. See? The chopper is coming back this way and looks like it's going to land."

Hope swelled in Alex's chest. The helicopter was returning and hovering close to the ground. But just when she thought it might land, the wind shifted, blowing smoke across the sky, blanketing the helicopter, hiding it and Jake from sight.

"Where'd they go?" Alex ran forward, her heart lodged in her throat.

A hand snagged her shoulder and pulled her back. "You can't run into that smoke."

"But I can't see Jake. Oh, sweet heaven, where'd he go?" she sobbed.

And then a break in the cloud of smoke and ash showed the helicopter hovering just above the ground, a black cloud whipping around it. Then the chopper shot back into the air and disappeared into the thick smoke.

The wind current shifted again, clearing the sky over Alex's head and carrying the smoke back over the pit.

The helicopter was nowhere to be seen in the night sky.

Suddenly, a loud crash sounded in the pit. Rotor blades broke off and flew out of the smoke, and a ball of flame lit up the sky.

Alex and Harm ran toward the edge of the pit and looked over into the flames rising up from the crashed helicopter.

"Jake!" Alex screamed. She would have leaped over the edge and slid down into the pit if Harm hadn't wrapped an arm around her waist and held on tight. "Let go! I have to find him."

"If he's down there, you don't want to find him. Aviation fuel burns hot. There won't be anything left to find."

"He can't be gone." Alex turned and buried her face against Harm's shirt. "I think I might love him," she sobbed.

"Alex!" a voice called out.

The sound cut through Alex's sobs. She looked up and blinked the tears from her eyes.

A tall man, covered in soot, walked out of the smoke toward her. "Alex?" He held open his arms.

Alex ran toward Jake, stumbling in her hurry, her tears falling again, blinding her with her joy. She slammed into him, knocking them both off their feet. Jake landed hard, but cushioned her fall.

He chuckled and coughed. "Hey, why the tears?" He pushed to a sitting position and gathered her in his arms. "Did you think I wasn't coming back?"

"Yes!" She grabbed his face between her palms and kissed him hard, then leaned back.

"I died a thousand deaths when you jumped on that skid. What were you thinking?"

He shrugged, a crooked smile making his teeth shine white against his blackened face. "I wasn't really thinking. I just acted."

"Don't do that again," she said.

"Yes, ma'am." He cupped the back of her head and kissed her thoroughly before letting her up for air. "I nearly died a thousand deaths when you went missing. Why did you leave T-Mac? He would have kept you safe. What were *you* thinking?"

She gave him a sheepish smile. "I wasn't really thinking. I just acted."

Jake shook his head. "We're a pair, the two of us."

She nodded. "Yeah, Big Jake. So, what are we going to do about it?"

"I guess we'll have to make a go of it." He hugged her tight. "I kind of got used to having you around on our little trek in the hills."

"Same here." She leaned her forehead against his. "Thank you for coming after me."

"Are you kidding?" Harm said as he walked over to them. "He was coming, with or without us." He held out a hand and helped Alex to her feet. "Sorry to break up this little reunion, but we have more work to do."

Jake rose to his feet, nodding. "Philburn or Whitley sent us a different set of coordinates to find you. We think it was a setup, sending us into a hotbed of ISIS. Our Special Forces counterparts are pre-positioned to launch an attack. We want to be there to help out."

Alex frowned. "And what about the people here?"

"Our guys have secured Philburn's guards and their weapons," Harm said. "We put out a call to our command to coordinate the transport of the conscripted workers. They will be returned to their villages."

With a sigh, Alex nodded. "Okay. I guess I'll let you go."

Harm laughed. "Mighty generous of you. T-Mac and some of the others are staying behind while the rest move out."

Though Alex wanted to ask why Jake couldn't stay, she bit down on her tongue. The SEALs had a mission and a method. She'd have to be patient.

"If all goes well, I'll see you back at the embassy in the morning." Jake pulled her into his arms and kissed her again. Then he set her away from him and followed Harm and a dozen SEALs to the clearing where three helicopters swooped in one by one. The men loaded into the choppers and they lifted off, the sound of the rotor blades fading into the night.

Alex drew in a deep breath and tried not to think about the new danger they'd be facing at their next rendezvous site.

All she could hope was that Harm was right and Jake would come up smelling like roses. In the meantime, her heart ached and her eyes stung, on the verge of more tears. She didn't have time for tears. She had work to do in order to help ensure the repatriation of the workers to the appropriate villages.

She glanced once more at the night sky where the helicopters had disappeared, and then went to work.

Chapter Eighteen

Jake hurried through the gate at the embassy, anxious to see Alex. He was dirty, covered in smoke and grime from a hard night's fight.

The coordinates Philburn and Whitley had given them had been as they suspected. The site was an ISIS militant camp. Thankfully, the Special Forces unit had done a good job of reconnaissance and hadn't been spotted by the rebels.

The mission had gone off with textbook accuracy. The ISIS fighters had been stockpiling munitions and explosives, and had been building improvised explosive devices in preparation for an attack on Niamey.

Not only had they stopped them from succeeding in a devastating blow to the capital city, but they'd also captured Abu Nuru al-Waseka, the leader of the Islamic State faction in Niger. The leader was more than willing to bring down those infidels who'd enlisted his assistance in stirring up trouble and finding free, able-bodied men to work the mine. He quickly named Quinten Philburn and Thomas Whitley as the Americans who'd paid him in weapons.

The debrief with Ambassador Brightbill and President Rafini had gone on for hours, but had finally ended.

Now all Jake wanted was to find Alex, get a shower and eat something. In that order.

He stopped in front of her door and knocked loudly.

When she didn't answer right away, he knocked again. Perhaps she'd gone out to eat, since it was well past noon and the sun had been up for hours. Or had she gone with the displaced workers to help them find their way back to their respective villages? In which case, he might miss her altogether.

That last thought had him frowning heavily. Now that their mission was complete—the ISIS rebels contained and the missionaries saved—they had no reason to stay in Niger. By the next morning, they would be redeployed to Djibouti and another mission in some other part of Africa.

Jake wanted to see Alex before he had to

leave. He didn't want to leave without talking to her. Hell, he didn't want to leave her at all. He had known her for such a short time, but it felt like a lifetime. He knew what he needed to know about her to realize she was special. The kind of woman he wanted in his life. No… She was the only woman he wanted in his life.

He couldn't leave without telling her that he wanted to see her again. Not just once, but a lot. How they would make that happen, he wasn't sure. But somehow he would, even if he had to spend all of his leave time flying back and forth to Niger to see her.

Once more he knocked on her door, but no one answered. Disappointed, he went to the room next door, let himself in and closed the door behind him.

"About time you realized I wasn't in my room," a soft voice said from the shadows.

Jake's heart lit up and he swung toward Alex.

She lay on her side on the bed, wearing a sexy nightgown and nothing else. Her shiny black hair hung down over her shoulders and her eyes sparkled.

He sighed. "Alex."

She slid her long legs over the side of the bed and padded barefoot to where he stood at the door. "Need some help getting out of that gear?"

He shook his head. "No. I'm filthy and you're not. Don't touch me until I've had a chance to shower."

"I don't care if I get dirty," she said. "You've seen me covered in dust and grime and in nothing at all. Let me help you." She reached out, unbuckled the clasps on his protective vest and slid it over his shoulders. When it dropped to the ground, a puff of dust and soot rose around it.

Jake gripped her shoulders and set her away from him. "There's nothing I want more than to hold you and let you touch me, but I need a shower first." He held up a finger. "Hold that thought and don't change a thing. I'll be right back." Then he ducked into the bathroom, stripped out of his clothes and jumped into the shower. He didn't care that the water coming out of the faucet started out icy cold; all he cared about was getting clean so he could hold Alex's perfect body against his.

As he soaped and lathered, a muddy, sooty stream of water swished off his body and down the drain. He squirted an entire trial-size bottle of shampoo into his hand and ran it through his hair and down over his arms and shoulders.

Then he ducked beneath the showerhead and rinsed.

"You missed a spot," Alex said behind him. Her hands reached around him for the bar of soap in the dish.

He turned to find her standing in the shower, naked and beautiful, her hands filled with soapy lather.

"Let me," she said, and ran her hands over every inch of his shoulders, back, chest and torso. As the water rinsed the soap away, she pressed kisses where her hands had been, working her way downward, her body and hair getting wetter as she went.

Her hands smoothed over his thighs, down past his knees to his ankles until she'd touched every part of his body but one.

Jake's shaft rose to the occasion, jutting straight and stiff. He wanted her so badly he could barely breathe.

She took him in her hands and stroked him until he felt like he'd explode.

Past his ability to contain himself, he bent, clasped her thighs in both hands, lifted her up and wrapped her legs around his waist. Then he marched out of the shower and bathroom and straight to the bed.

She laughed. "Aren't we going to dry off?" She kissed his cheek and nibbled on his earlobe.

"Can't," he said.

"We'll get the sheets all wet," she said, clinging to him as he tried to lay her on the bed.

"Don't care," he replied. Since she wouldn't let go of his neck so he could lay her down, he turned his back to the bed and lay down with her still in his arms.

Alex slid her legs down his, wet, warm and delicious. "You're a man who knows what he wants."

"I am. And I want you." He kissed her and then flipped her over onto her back. "When we're apart, all I can think about is being back with you." He stared down into her gaze. Though he was desperate to plunge into her, he wanted her to see the sincerity in his eyes. "I'm not into one-night stands."

"Neither am I." She reached up and cupped his cheek. "So, what are we doing here?"

"Starting something that I hope will last a lifetime," he said.

Her eyes glistened with unshed tears. "You don't think it's too soon to feel this way?"

He shook his head. "I knew the moment I found you in the village coming back to help the missionaries."

Her lips trembled as a smile pulled at the corners. A single tear slid from the edge of one eye. "I didn't know until you held me in your arms in that cave."

"It's not a contest, woman. I want you in my life."

She gave him a watery smile. "And I want to be in your life."

"I have a dangerous job."

"I won't always like it, but I know it means a lot to you." She brushed her thumb across his lips. "I'll be there when you come home."

"You'd give up Africa?"

She smiled. "I'd give up breathing if I could be with you even some of the time."

"Please," he said, and bent to kiss her lips. "Don't give up breathing. I need you too much. Can we make this work?"

She nodded. "Look how far we've come in just a few short days. The rest of our lives will be a piece of cake." She wrapped her arms around him and pulled his mouth to hers.

"Is this what love feels like?" he asked against her mouth.

"I'm pretty sure it is." She reached a hand over to the nightstand and grabbed a foil packet. "Now, if we're done talking, I'd like a little more action."

Jake laughed out loud. "A woman after my own heart." He made quick work of the protection and slid into her, feeling as if he'd finally come home. Whatever the next day brought, he and Alex would find a way to be together. No matter how hard the task. As always, for any SEAL, the only easy day was yesterday.

* * * * *

Get 4 FREE REWARDS!

We'll send you 2 FREE Books
<u>plus</u> 2 FREE Mystery Gifts.

Harlequin® Romantic Suspense books feature heart-racing sensuality and the promise of a sweeping romance set against the backdrop of suspense.

FREE
Value Over
$20

YES! Please send me 2 FREE Harlequin® Romantic Suspense novels and my 2 FREE gifts (gifts are worth about $10 retail). After receiving them, if I don't wish to receive any more books, I can return the shipping statement marked "cancel." If I don't cancel, I will receive 4 brand-new novels every month and be billed just $4.99 per book in the U.S. or $5.74 per book in Canada. That's a savings of at least 12% off the cover price! It's quite a bargain! Shipping and handling is just 50¢ per book in the U.S. and 75¢ per book in Canada.* I understand that accepting the 2 free books and gifts places me under no obligation to buy anything. I can always return a shipment and cancel at any time. The free books and gifts are mine to keep no matter what I decide.

240/340 HDN GMYZ

Name (please print)

Address   Apt. #

City   State/Province   Zip/Postal Code

Mail to the **Reader Service:**
IN U.S.A.: P.O. Box 1341, Buffalo, NY 14240-8531
IN CANADA: P.O. Box 603, Fort Erie, Ontario L2A 5X3

Want to try 2 free books from another series! Call 1-800-873-8635 or visit www.ReaderService.com.

HRS19

Get 4 FREE REWARDS!

We'll send you 2 FREE Books plus 2 FREE Mystery Gifts.

Harlequin Presents® books feature a sensational and sophisticated world of international romance where sinfully tempting heroes ignite passion.

FREE Value Over **$20**

Get 4 FREE REWARDS!

We'll send you 2 FREE Books <u>plus</u> 2 FREE Mystery Gifts.

FREE Value Over **$20**

Both the **Romance** and **Suspense** collections feature compelling novels written by many of today's best-selling authors.

YES! Please send me 2 FREE novels from the Essential Romance or Essential Suspense Collection and my 2 FREE gifts (gifts are worth about $10 retail). After receiving them, if I don't wish to receive any more books, I can return the shipping statement marked "cancel." If I don't cancel, I will receive 4 brand-new novels every month and be billed just $6.74 each in the U.S. or $7.24 each in Canada. That's a savings of at least 16% off the cover price. It's quite a bargain! Shipping and handling is just 50¢ per book in the U.S. and 75¢ per book in Canada.* I understand that accepting the 2 free books and gifts places me under no obligation to buy anything. I can always return a shipment and cancel at any time. The free books and gifts are mine to keep no matter what I decide.

Choose one: ☐ **Essential Romance**
(194/394 MDN GMY7)

☐ **Essential Suspense**
(191/391 MDN GMY7)

Name (please print)

Address   Apt. #

City   State/Province   Zip/Postal Code

Mail to the **Reader Service:**
IN U.S.A.: P.O. Box 1341, Buffalo, NY 14240-8531
IN CANADA: P.O. Box 603, Fort Erie, Ontario L2A 5X3

Want to try 2 free books from another series? Call 1-800-873-8635 or visit www.ReaderService.com.